Lycos wa purpose in his steps now.

He wanted to see her closer. As he approached, stepping across the cobbled courtyard, he saw her poised more tensely yet—as if for flight, or fight.

"Are you lost?" she asked again. He could hear the tension in her voice, the potential alarm. He halted.

"Lost? No—not if this is the *Mas Delfine*?"

He saw her eyes widen even more, alarm now evident, and confusion. Absently he noticed now, closer to her as he was, that her eyes were a vivid shade of blue, fringed by smoky lashes. His own dark eyes washed over her, taking her in. Whatever he'd expected to find here, if he'd expected anything at all, it was not a woman like this.

So breath-catchingly lovely...

"What...what do you want with the *Mas Delfine, monsieur*?" she was saying, and now there was more than alarm in her voice.

He lifted one eyebrow in slight, silent mockery.

"I want to take possession of it, *mademoiselle*," he echoed the formality of her address to him. "It happens to be mine."

Julia James lives in England and adores the peaceful verdant countryside and the wild shores of Cornwall. She also loves the Mediterranean—so rich in myth and history, with its sunbaked landscapes and olive groves, ancient ruins and azure seas. "The perfect setting for romance!" she says. "Rivaled only by the lush tropical heat of the Caribbean—palms swaying by a silver-sand beach lapped by turquoise waters... What more could lovers want?"

Books by Julia James

Harlequin Presents

Irresistible Bargain with the Greek
The Greek's Duty-Bound Royal Bride
The Greek's Penniless Cinderella
Cinderella in the Boss's Palazzo
Cinderella's Baby Confession
Destitute Until the Italian's Diamond
The Cost of Cinderella's Confession
Reclaimed by His Billion-Dollar Ring
Contracted as the Italian's Bride
The Heir She Kept from the Billionaire
Greek's Temporary Cinderella
Vows of Revenge
Accidental One-Night Baby
Marriage Made in Hate

Visit the Author Profile page at Harlequin.com for more titles.

DIMISTRIOS'S BOUGHT MISTRESS

JULIA JAMES

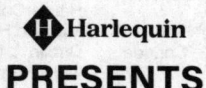

PRESENTS

If you purchased this book without a cover you should be aware that this book is stolen property. It was reported as "unsold and destroyed" to the publisher, and neither the author nor the publisher has received any payment for this "stripped book."

Recycling programs for this product may not exist in your area.

ISBN-13: 978-1-335-21338-9

Dimistrios's Bought Mistress

Copyright © 2025 by Julia James

All rights reserved. No part of this book may be used or reproduced in any manner whatsoever without written permission.

Without limiting the author's and publisher's exclusive rights, any unauthorized use of this publication to train generative artificial intelligence (AI) technologies is expressly prohibited.

This is a work of fiction. Names, characters, places and incidents are either the product of the author's imagination or are used fictitiously. Any resemblance to actual persons, living or dead, businesses, companies, events or locales is entirely coincidental.

For questions and comments about the quality of this book, please contact us at CustomerService@Harlequin.com.

TM and ® are trademarks of Harlequin Enterprises ULC.

Harlequin Enterprises ULC
22 Adelaide St. West, 41st Floor
Toronto, Ontario M5H 4E3, Canada
www.Harlequin.com

HarperCollins Publishers
Macken House, 39/40 Mayor Street Upper,
Dublin 1, D01 C9W8, Ireland
www.HarperCollins.com

Printed in Lithuania

DIMISTRIOS'S BOUGHT MISTRESS

For race horses, and greyhounds, everywhere—
for their happy retirement after racing.

PROLOGUE

THERE WAS COMPLETE silence in the room. It was not a large room, more of a *salon* privé, and it was dominated by the baize-covered table around which the players were sitting. For a moment, the scene held like a living tableau. The croupier sat in his position, quite motionless, face professionally blank. Players holding their cards with piles of chips and rolls of cash of assorted sizes in front of them. And sitting in the centre of the table was a loose heap of chips and cash, reaching sky-high denominations, along with a hand written note.

The only two players with hands still being played stared at each other across the table. One of the players held his cards in a grip so tight that his nails had left indentations in them. The tension in him was reflected vividly in his reddened, puffy cheeks, the venomous stare in his pouched eyes and the press of his fleshy lips.

The other player was leaning back in his gilt chair, holding his cards with nothing showing in his face. He might have been a stone statue carved by a master sculptor who had delineated the hard planes of his high cheekbones, the blade of his nose, the compressed line of his mouth and the chiselled line of his jaw, shadowing now once more at this late hour. Only his eyes could not have been captured by the sculptor. Half-lidded, very slightly narrowed and dark as night. And with no emotion showing in them. Nothing at all.

'Messieurs?'

The neutral prompt by the croupier made the tenser of the players clench his cards tightly with a jerk. His expression changed. He saw the chance to make a greedy, triumphant thrust at his opponent. He put down his hand.

A subliminal collective murmuration came from the other players present and, as one, their eyes turned to the other player. For a microsecond, even a microsecond of a microsecond, he still did not move. The look of greedy triumph in the other man's face intensified. Behind the triumph was another expression—relief. Sweat visibly beaded on his brow. A pulse throbbed at his neck.

Then his opponent, with a movement so slight he might only have been flicking a speck of dust from the table, laid down his hand. There was still nothing in his eyes. Nothing at all.

An audible gasp sounded from those watching and an audible murmur of disbelief came from one.

'The Wolf wins—again.'

CHAPTER ONE

Earlier that day

ARIELLE STOOD FROM where she had been crouched deadheading the vivid, vermillion geraniums. They grew in terracotta pots lining the low wall that separated the wide paved terrace in front of the house from the garden beyond. The garden itself was rich with Provençal beauty, from the glossy dark leaves of the oleanders and olive trees framing the space, to the citrus, peach and mulberry trees behind. Arielle's gaze swept over the vista. A garden bathed in the warm, late afternoon sunshine. So familiar. So loved. And so soon to be lost.

How will I bear it?

The thought made her heart clench but she crushed it down.

All I can do is make the very most, while I can, of my beloved home.

Before it was sold.

Because sold it would be. Her stepbrother, Gerald, would see to it. So would his mother—Arielle's stepmother. Arielle's eyes darkened. A woman more different from her own unworldly, gentle mother, her father's first wife, was impossible to imagine. Naomi was as hard as nails and avaricious to the core. Her one soft spot was for her detestable son, Gerald. She doted on him, indulged him, funded him. Not with her own money of course, but with her husbands'. *Husbands, plural* Arielle thought bitterly.

Naomi's third husband had been Arielle's father, Charles Frobisher.

He had made his money in property—making him wealthy enough to tempt Naomi Maitland to get her claws into him when he'd been widowed. When he'd shockingly succumbed to a heart attack eighteen months previously, Arielle had discovered that in his new will he'd left everything he'd possessed to Naomi. His daughter had inherited nothing.

The clenching of her heart was like a vice now as Arielle's eyes swept round, up from the garden and over to the house behind it. The beautiful, honey-coloured old stone Provençal farmhouse, with its tiled roof and its wooden-shuttered windows. The house she loved, so, so much. The *Mas Delfine*.

It had been her mother's house, inherited down the generations, but had become the property of Arielle's stepmother. Bestowed upon Naomi by Arielle's own father.

How could he do it to me? How?

Unlike the close relationship she'd had with her mother, Arielle had never been as close to her father, focussed as he was on amassing the wealth he'd made in property. But she had been his only child and he'd been casually affectionate towards her. She'd always understood that the *mas* she'd loved so much, where she had spent the summer holidays with her mother from boarding school in England, would one day come to her, passing down the female line.

But when her mother had died, so tragically three years ago, she'd discovered that the *mas* was actually her father's property. Even then, she had assumed that her father would leave it to her, his daughter. But it had gone to Naomi, along with the rest of his estate. Naomi had then promptly bestowed the house upon the son she doted on. Whereupon Gerald had spitefully informed Arielle that he would sell it as soon as he could find a buyer who would pay the price he wanted for it and there would be nothing, absolutely nothing, she could do about it.

But until that happened…

Until then I will stay here, with my memories, and make the most of this time. My last summer—

Anguish made her heart clench again.

Lycos Dimistrios strolled out of the casino. A mix of satisfaction and contempt filled him. It was a familiar combination. One that had been known to him since he had first embarked upon his ascent from poverty to the world he now lived in—the world of the rich. He glanced over the scene in front of him. The seafront promenade here on the French Riviera overlooked a marina that was filled with luxury yachts, all glittering with lights and throbbing with the sounds from the onboard parties still going at this hour, gone midnight.

As Lycos waited for his valet-parked car to arrive he was conscious of the folded piece of paper in the inner pocket of his tuxedo jacket. It might have been an unusual win, but a notary would find it all in order. Lycos had made sure of that.

His opponent had been a fool, but then so were many who chose to play him. This one had been particularly repellent—boastful, rude to the croupier, rude to the waiters, demanding and entitled. The kind of person who liked to win simply to beat someone else down. Especially, this evening. Lycos's lip curled.

Lycos was known on the casino circuit as 'The Wolf'. His nickname was a play on his name in Greek and, as his formidable reputation had grown, the name had been deemed appropriate. It was a reputation he had earned.

Those who indulged in gambling did so for a variety of reasons—but Lycos had just one. To make money. Make it and keep it. Every gambling win he'd ever made had gone, apart from retaining what he would stake in his next play, into solid wealth. Wealth that had been stored, accumulated and invested. Taking him far, far away from his lowly origins in the backstreets of Athens.

Now his world was very different. The fabled, glitzy Côte d'Azur or anywhere else that boasted opportunities for gaming at his level. Anywhere that the wealthy gathered to disport themselves expensively. He disposed his time among them, going where the mood and impulse took him.

Right now it was taking him north as his regular review of his investments, managed for him by a prestigious private bank based in Paris, was due. His car was drawing up with his case already in the boot. Bestowing an appropriate note from his wallet, he took the driving seat, loosened his black tie and unfastened the top button of his dress shirt. Despite the lateness of the hour, he was as sober as a judge. He never touched alcohol when he was at the tables.

Gunning the engine, he moved out into the traffic, heading inland. Heading for Paris.

Arielle turned over in her sleep. The light night breeze from her wide-open bedroom window played over her eyelids. She was dreaming. A dream of happier times, when her mother was still alive and Arielle had had no idea that she would lose her so soon. When she'd had no idea that she would lose her beloved home as well. A slight smile curved her lips, her long hair flowing over the pillowcase.

Outside the stars burned in the dark velvet sky, wheeling in their timeless arc, ushering the land towards the coming dawn.

The dawn that would bring the day that would take her home from her and change Arielle's life for ever.

The sky was starting to lighten in the east, the night was fading. Lycos changed gear as the powerful car steadily ate up the miles along the Rhône valley, heading north. A road sign loomed up in front of him, indicating an upcoming turning, and he frowned slightly. Why did it seem familiar? Then it clicked. That was the town, Saint-Clément, scrawled as part of the address written on the piece of paper in his jacket pocket.

Another sign for the town flashed past and as the turning approached Lycos moved with a sudden impulse. He was in no rush to reach Paris. He could afford a detour. He turned off Route 7, pausing only to reset his sat nav—he would not rely on road signage alone in this unfamiliar part of the country.

Nearly an hour later he was glad he'd had the sat nav to guide him. He'd gone past the town he'd made the turning for and headed out into the open countryside, which was bathed in dawn light. He was aiming for the location in the next line of the address, a much smaller village, still some distance away.

He almost regretted his impulse but not quite. The Provençal landscape was beautiful at this early hour, washed in the palest dawn sunlight, as he passed cypress trees, olive groves, vineyards and citrus stands, with occasional houses and farms dotting the undulating terrain. The road narrowed so he slowed down although there was no other traffic on the road this early.

In grassy, stone-walled fields cows lifted their heads incuriously, sheep and goats ignored him and the occasional rabbit darted away. Mist hung in low hollows giving the countryside a mythical feel, ancient and timeless, and roadside flowers coloured the verges.

Finally he reached the small village he had been looking for. The little square with its sandy, tree-edged area for boules was deserted but Lycos spotted a *boulangerie* with its door open. Suddenly hungry, he pulled up to buy a freshly-baked baguette and half a dozen croissants. Checking the directions to his destination, which was still a good few kilometres away, he resumed his journey, demolishing two of the croissants in short order.

The road had narrowed further and had started to

climb. Lycos slid his window down—the air was sweet and fresh, and had already begun to warm up. He propped his elbow on the opened window and kept his speed low from necessity. Absently he rubbed his jaw. He needed a shave and a shower. And to get out of his tuxedo into something more appropriate for the day. He would make use of the facilities at his destination. His newest acquisition.

Not that he'd keep it long. He'd check it out, then hand it over to realtors to be disposed of for its maximum value.

He had no use for a farmhouse in the middle of Provence.

Arielle stepped through the kitchen door into the courtyard. It was cobbled, with a gateway set in one wall that was wide enough for a car or farm cart. There was a row of barns opposite, one of which she used as a garage for her ancient but still roadworthy car, the others for general storage and her poultry. Inset into the wall facing the gateway was a much narrower wooden gate that led through to the gardens. She headed through the narrower gate, picking up the two watering cans that she'd filled the previous evening, to water the pots against the day's later heat, part of the slow rhythm of life here at the *mas*. Though money was tight, she was grateful that the money her father had given to her when she turned eighteen to fund her music studies allowed her to live here—albeit modestly.

Until Gerald sells it.

No, she would not spoil her peaceful mood by thinking of that. She carried on with the watering, glancing fondly at her beloved home with the morning sunshine glancing off the French windows leading into the parlour. Not grand enough to be a drawing room, nevertheless, she loved its old-fashioned charm, with its stone fireplace, worn but comfortable sofas and chairs, old wooden painted armoire against one wall, and some not very good but familiar and well-loved paintings on the walls in their faded gilt frames. In pride of place was her piano. A baby grand that had been a gift from her father when she had been accepted into music college seven years previously.

Watering done, she stood for a moment enjoying the quietness. She wasn't yet dressed, but the cotton, belted dressing gown she wore over her nightshirt was fine to eat breakfast in. There was no one to see her and, unless she went into the village, or called on her nearest neighbours who lived on another farmstead a good kilometre away, she wouldn't see anyone from one day to the next. She liked it that way. Who knew she would be forced to leave the *mas*?

She gave an instinctive shiver, despite the morning warmth, and went back into the courtyard. The next task was to let out the poultry and feed them before having breakfast at the ironwork table on the terrace in front of the parlour.

Then, abruptly, she paused, frowning. The sound of a car engine along the lane reached her. It was an unusual sound at the best of times, for the country lane led only to *Mas Delfine*. The engine note grew louder and she stared through the open gateway to see a vehicle approaching slowly over the stony, uneven surface. It was a vehicle such as she had never seen anywhere near the *mas*. Completely unsuitable for the narrow lanes and completely out of place here. Low, lean, black and very, very clearly an extremely expensive supercar.

What on earth?

The car nosed, engine growling, up to the gateway then stopped, the engine cutting out. The driver's door opened and a man got out, looking about him as he slammed the car door shut. The noise reverberated in the silent air like a gunshot.

Arielle clutched at the lapels of her dressing gown. Fear crabbed in her stomach.

Then, reason fought it down. The driver was obviously lost. There was no other explanation for him having turned up here. Not just in a car like that but also, she realised, dressed in, of all things, a tuxedo. God alone knew where he'd come from—maybe some grand château had hosted a flash party and he'd got lost leaving?

He continued to look around him at the front of the *mas*, visible from where he'd pulled up, and she studied him a moment. He was tall, dark-haired and, though she could not see his face well, his profile seemed to show him frowning. Obviously wondering where on earth he'd arrived at by mistake. She had best put him to rights and send him on his way.

Taking a breath, she headed towards him, her soft-soled slippers making no sound on the cobbles. In the open gateway she paused.

'Can I help you?' she asked, speaking French.

The man's head whipped round, focussing laser eyes on her. For a second he did not speak. Nor could she.

Arielle's lungs seemed suddenly empty of air. Her

gaze fixed on him. She could feel her fingers clutch more tightly at her lapels as she stared. Stared at the most incredible looking man she had ever seen in her life...

Lycos did not move. His gaze rested on the woman standing there. Slender, wearing nothing but a thin, pale blue cotton dressing gown with a cross-over belt that distinctly displayed her shapely figure. Her dark hair tumbled down over her shoulders and waved back from her face. A face that made his gaze even more keen. Oval-shaped, with a tender mouth, peach soft cheeks, delicate arched eyebrows set over deep set eyes. Eyes that were wide and startled.

He started to walk towards her and saw her take a half step back. He saw her hands, with their long fingers and unvarnished nails, clutch more tightly at her lapels.

'Can I help you?' she said again. 'Are you lost?'

Lost? The word echoed meaninglessly in Lycos's head. No, he was not lost—

Or was he?

He continued to walk towards her, a purpose in his steps now. He wanted to see her up close. As he approached, stepping across the cobbled courtyard, he saw her poised more tensely yet.

'Are you lost?' she asked again. This time she addressed him in English, a frown of puzzlement on her face.

'Lost?' he echoed, matching her English. 'No—not if this is the *Mas Delfine*?'

He saw her eyes widen even more, alarm now evident and confusion. Absently he noticed now, closer to her as he was, that her eyes were a vivid shade of blue, fringed by smoky lashes. His own dark eyes washed over her, taking her in. Whatever he'd expected to find here, if he'd expected anything at all, it was not a woman like this.

So breathtakingly lovely...

She was speaking again and he made himself focus on what she was saying, not her loveliness as she stood there illuminated by the early morning sun that bathed her in its light.

'What...what do you want with the *Mas Delfine, monsieur*?' she was saying, sticking to English. Now there was more than alarm in her voice.

Lycos let his eyes rest on her. Whoever she was and however lovely she was standing there—graceful, beautiful and *deshabille* with her dressing gown, tumbling hair and blue, blue eyes—it was time to make something clear to her.

'I want to take possession of it, *mademoiselle*,' he said echoing the formality of her address to him. 'It happens to be mine.'

CHAPTER TWO

ARIELLE HEARD HIS WORDS. Heard them but could not comprehend them. Could not bear to. Oh, dear God, had it happened then, was Gerald finally carrying out his threat? She felt faintness drumming in her ears. Her vision blurred. Her body swayed and folded.

She heard the man mutter an oath, in a language she did not understand, but her hearing was dimming. Clouds rolled up to smother her, suffocate her, thrust her down, down, down...

And then she was steadied. An arm snaked around her waist, holding her upright by force, all but carrying her across to the bench beside the kitchen door. She was lowered gently to the bench. A hand was at the nape of her neck, pressing her head towards her knees. Slowly, slowly, the drumming in her ears faded and her senses returned. She began to lift her head and instantly the hand at her nape was lifted away. She swallowed, sitting upright slowly, turning her head towards the man sitting beside her. She blinked blindly.

'Who...who are you?' The faintness might be passing, but it was in her voice still, almost a stammer.

Her eyes went to him. He was close—far, far too

close—and she could see his face fully now. A narrow face with a hard jaw that was rough-edged with stubble, high cheekbones, dark eyebrows and even darker eyes.

Eyes that she could have drowned in.

Eyes that were studying her with a piercing gaze.

He sat back, reaching inside his jacket pocket. He slid out a silver card case and extracted a card from it. Not once, not even for a moment, did he take his eyes from her.

She took the card in her nerveless fingers. *Lycos Dimistrios.* That was all it said. She lifted her head to stare at him blankly.

Greek, she thought even more blankly, *he's Greek—*

He got to his feet, removed his card from her numb fingers and dropped it casually into the outer pocket of his tuxedo jacket. Arielle found herself wondering, with that same strange detachment, why he was wearing a tuxedo. Why his bow tie was undone, hanging loosely either side of his open top button of his dress shirt. Why the effect seemed to make her want to go on gazing at him as he stood there tall, dark against the sun, looking down at her with that unreadable expression on his face with his piercing dark eyes, roughened jawline, well-shaped mouth....

Inside her chest she felt, as if from very far away, her heart starting to thud. She realised he was speaking, still in English.

'So now you know my name, tell me yours. Who are you?'

She got to her feet.

'I am Arielle Degrange Frobisher,' she said. Her head straightened and she looked at him directly. She continued speaking with quiet dignity and resolve, '*Mas Delfine* is my home. It has been...' she took a breath, never letting her eyes drop from his '...my mother's family home for over two hundred years and it has been stolen from me.'

Nothing changed on Lycos's face.

'Is that so?' he said. His voice was expressionless. Something was playing out here and he wanted to know what it was without showing his hand. He never showed his hand...

He saw her shoulders go back. 'Yes,' she said. 'It is so. And, whatever claim my...stepbrother has made that it is his, it is not. Nor is he free to dispose of it.'

Her voice was calm as she spoke, but Lycos could hear the emotions in it. The anger. The rage. The fear.

His thoughts ran silently but rapidly behind his levelling eyes. Was she telling the truth? Was ownership of the *mas* disputed? If so, there would be, shortly, a reckoning that would be of extreme discomfort to the man he had faced down at the casino the previous night. He frowned inwardly. Stepbrother, she'd said?

'Gerald Maitland is your stepbrother?'

She nodded. 'You know him? Or did you deal only with his agents?'

His mouth formed a faint, caustic smile that had not a ghost of humour in it.

'With him. Personally,' he said. He did not attempt to hide the edge in his voice.

Her eyes widened and he could see she was about to speak. Peremptorily he lifted a hand.

'Later,' he said. 'We will discuss this later. For now...' he dropped the edge in his voice and became matter of fact, '...I require the use of a bathroom, preferably en-suite. And then breakfast.'

He turned away, not caring about her reaction to his list of immediate requirements, and strode back to his car. He unloaded his suitcase, retrieved the baguette and the bag of remaining croissants, and returned to where she stood in the cobbled courtyard, still bathed in sunlight. His eyes narrowed slightly, assessing her.

She really was so very lovely, standing there like that in the faded cotton dressing gown with her tumbling long dark hair and those incredible blue eyes.

Even though in there was nothing in her eyes but shock and anger.

Suddenly Lycos didn't want to see that expression there. He held up the baguette and the paper bag, then deposited them on the bench.

'For breakfast,' he said. 'We shall discuss the situation then. Now, show me to my room if you please.'

He guided her inside, into a large, old-fashioned kitchen. For a moment he thought she was going to balk but then, with the same quiet dignity with which she had told him who she was, she complied. She led the way through into a wide entrance hall with what he assumed was the front door to the *mas* and from which a stone staircase led to the upper storey.

'You can use the room at the far end of the landing to the right,' she told him expressionlessly. 'The bathroom is next door. The water is hot at this hour as long as you do not use too much of it.'

She walked back into the kitchen, shutting the door to the hallway. For a moment Lycos looked at the closed door, as if he might want to see through it, then he headed upstairs with thoughts arranging and rearranging themselves inside his head.

Arielle waited until, some minutes later, she could hear the sound of the shower running through the rumbling, ancient pipework. Then, swiftly, she ran upstairs to the sanctuary of her own bedroom.

But what sanctuary was it now? How could it be?

The numbness, which had overtaken her since she had so nearly passed out with shock, had left her and now only shock remained. Shock and anger and anguish.

How can I bear it? To lose my home? My heritage— my birthright?

She shook with the intensity of her emotions. She'd been through it all with the lawyers and now, this very day, the blow she had dreaded for so long had finally fallen.

She gave a smothered cry, hurrying herself into her clothes with shaking hands. She pulled open her bedroom door cautiously and peered out along the landing. The shower had stopped. Maybe he was shaving now, this man who had come to take her home from her.

His image flashed into her head. He'd needed a shave, badly.

He looked like a pirate.

But that was what he was, wasn't it? This Lycos Dimistrios, a pirate who seized the property of others. Who helped himself to it.

***

Lycos snapped open the lid of his suitcase, which he'd lifted onto the bed. It was an old-fashioned bed with a metal frame and a thick mattress that was covered with a quilt. The furniture was equally old-fashioned. A sturdy wooden dressing table, a large wooden wardrobe and a pair of straw-seated upright chairs. Knotted rugs lay either side of the wide bed and the rest of the floor was bare wooden boards that had been polished smooth over the years. Flowered curtains hung either side of the window. He opened the window to let in fresh air and the curtains rustled in the warm breeze. He sifted through his clothes and selected a polo shirt and casual chinos. He slipped on the chinos, dropping the thin towel he'd found in the bathroom—as old-fashioned as the bedroom, though sufficiently functional for his needs—from around his hips. As he pulled the polo shirt down over his torso he wandered to the window. The morning was heating up. He wondered if the place had a pool. A swim might be welcome later.

He frowned. Later? Was there going to be a later? Wasn't he simply going to eat, get shown round the place—however unwillingly—and then set off for Paris again? The interruption to his journey being as brief as that?

He stood, thoughts revolving, looking out of the window. It overlooked the rear of the house, out over the garden. Or should that be gardens, plural? They seemed extensive, sloping down through a couple of terraced levels to a hedge, beyond which seemed to be a field of lavender. He caught a whiff of the fragrance, borne towards him on the light breeze. To either side of the gardens were trees—citrus from the look of them and mulberry—creating a sheltered seclusion. Bougainvillea tumbled over low walls separating the terraced levels. Oleanders and olive trees lined the far edge of the next level. And immediately below his window, a wide stone-paved terrace was dotted with a multitude of terracotta pots bearing vividly hued geraniums. Another scent caught at him, besides that of lavender on the breeze. Coffee. He glanced sideways, taking in an ironwork table, shaded by a faded striped awning pulled out from the wall of the house above a pair of French windows. Breakfast was being set out for him.

He turned away, hungry suddenly. The two croissants he'd demolished en route from the village seemed a long time ago, and completely inadequate.

He wanted to eat. He wanted to see his new possession. And most of all, he realised with a mixture of self-mockery, purely masculine anticipation and something he could not identify so dismissed accordingly, he wanted to see the woman who said she still owned what he had, as it happened, acquired for himself.

Acquired on the turn of a card.

Like everything else he owned.

And now he owned this place too.

Arielle slid open the barn doors. The hens, followed by the ducks, surged out hungrily. She fetched their feed from the feedstore, added it to a bowl and took it to their pecking ground on the rough area beside the barns beyond the gateway. Averting her eyes from the monstrous car pulled up on the drive, she felt emotion stab.

Tight-mouthed, she went back into the kitchen, snatching up the baguette and bag of croissants from the bench as she passed it. She was in no mood to lift a finger over breakfast for the man who was taking her home from her, but alienating him might not be wise. He might order her to leave immediately, without time to make her preparations. Without time to pack up her belongings, arrange for the poultry to go to her neighbours and send her piano to the local *lycée*.

So she put the coffee on, sliced up the baguette and set it out with the croissants, put out some butter and apricot jam, heated the milk, set crockery and cutlery on a large tray, and then carried it all through to the parlour and then out to the terrace.

She stopped dead. He was already by the ironwork table, this Lycos Dimistrios whoever he was. She neither knew nor cared. But it was impossible not to let her gaze go to him and not just because of the threat he presented. No, it was quite a different reason.

Dressed in his tuxedo, with his open-necked dress shirt, loosened black tie and the darkly shadowed jawline, he'd looked a mix of elegant and decidedly rough. It had done things to her she'd had no business experiencing, let alone acknowledging. Now, though, his image was quite different. His jaw was smooth. His hair, still damp from his shower, feathered across his brow and his torso was sleekly contained within a dark blue polo shirt that moulded a clearly muscled chest and shoulders. A leather-strapped watch snaked around one wrist, echoing the leather belt on his pale chinos snaking around his lean hips. He looked expensively, casually devastating and she felt an entirely inappropriate hollow start up in her as she reacted with an entirely irrelevant female response.

One thing, though, had not changed—the piercing gaze aimed at her from his unreadable dark eyes.

Though her tee shirt was baggy and her cut offs revealed nothing of her legs but her calves, she felt suddenly undressed.

For a moment he said nothing and nor did she. Then, abruptly, Arielle deposited the tray on the table and proceeded to unload it. As she did, he pulled out an iron chair and sat himself down.

'That coffee smells good, but is there no juice?' he asked, reaching for the basket with the baguette and croissants and helping himself.

Without a word, Arielle went back inside. In the kitchen she lifted four oranges from their bowl on the dresser, juiced them manually, poured the results into a glass and carried it back out. Silently, she put the glass down in front of him.

He glanced at her, busy with buttering his bread, then reached for the jar of apricot jam.

'*Merci*,' he said absently as he examined the jam jar. 'This looks home-made.'

Arielle sat down. 'A neighbour makes it. She grows a lot of apricots. I swap it for marmalade, as I grow a lot of oranges. As you can tell from the fresh juice.'

He lifted the glass and drank from it. 'That's good,' he said and nodded.

'I'm so glad it meets your approval,' Arielle said sweetly.

His glance pierced her. 'Considering they are my orange trees that is just as well,' he said.

She made no attempt to answer. After breakfast would come a conversation she could not avoid. She felt as if claws of emotions had gripped her stomach—fear and dread.

She reached for a croissant, poured herself a coffee with hot milk, then dipped the croissant in it.

'I take mine black,' Lycos Dimistrios said, demolishing another slice of baguette and jam.

'Help yourself,' she invited, with the same acidic sweetness.

One dark eyebrow lifted. 'Just to the coffee?' he rejoined tauntingly.

Arielle's mouth tightened. She ignored him as he filled his cup and took a mouthful. Instead, she stared out over the gardens. Emotion rose like a tidal wave within her, but she fought it down. She found herself blinking, trying to fight the feelings.

'Tell me,' he said, his voice penetrating her grief. 'Why do you believe the *Mas Delfine* is yours? That it was stolen from you by your stepbrother?'

She turned to look at him.

'It was my stepmother who stole it. She persuaded my father to leave it to her. He died eighteen months ago.'

Her voice was steady, but it was hard for her to say it out loud, even now, and to acknowledge a betrayal of trust that was still hard to believe.

A faint frown appeared on Lycos Dimistrios's brow.

'You told me it belonged to your own mother. French law gives you a right to inherit. So, what happened?'

She took a breath, abandoning her croissant, and looked straight across at him—this marauder who'd turned up here to take from her what was hers by right.

'The *mas*...' she began, '...was my mother's and her mother's before her. It's been in my family for over two hundred years. But when my mother met my father there were debts on the property. My mother hoped my father would pay off the debts once they were married, but instead he made her a different offer. He suggested she actually sell him the *mas*, before she married him, because the sale price would clear the debts. He pointed out that he would then leave the *mas* to the children they would have. So, my mother agreed. My father became the legal owner of the property and my mother was confident that, naturally, it would one day pass to me as their only child.'

She reached for her coffee, needing its support. She was doing her best to keep her voice steady, unemotional, but she could feel the old tide of anger and hurt rising up inside her.

'But when my mother died three years ago, my father remarried. To my stepbrother's mother, Naomi. When my father died, eighteen months ago, I discovered...' her voice wobbled, and she had to fight it, '...that he had left everything to Naomi in his will. Everything.'

She steadied her voice with an effort.

'My father was English. His estate was English. The will had been proved under English law. I fought and fought it. But he owned the *mas*. As he'd bought it outright from my mother, it was his to dispose of as he wished. And he wished for Naomi to have it.'

Lycos frowned.

'Why?'

Anger burned in Arielle's eyes, a familiar and bitter feeling.

'Because she is a manipulative gold-digger who ran rings around my father and got everything he possessed! She dotes on her son and she's given him the *mas*. Now he intends to sell it—'

She caught herself.

'And now he has sold it.' Her voice was hollow.

She saw his dark head shake.

'Not quite.' He said in a dry voice.

Arielle stared at him as he continued to speak.

'He didn't sell it to me. I won it from him last night in a game of cards. It was all he had left to stake.'

CHAPTER THREE

Lycos saw her face pale.

'You *won* it from Gerald?'

'Yes. He was angry that I'd won every game and he stupidly let his anger get the better of him. Then he played badly, recklessly, which is always a sign of stupidity.' Lycos didn't bother to hide the contempt in his voice. 'And I took advantage of it.' He took a breath. 'So, the *Mas Delfine* is now mine.'

'It can't be! Not like that!' There was disbelief in her voice, as well as outrage and dismay.

He shrugged and said, 'It's legal. I made sure of it. The transfer of ownership was signed and witnessed. The formal paperwork will follow.' He let his eyes rest on her impassively. 'Why object? If I hadn't won it off him he'd have sold it anyway, so you'd be the loser still. What's it to you who owns it now or how they acquired it?'

Something glimmered in those deep blue eyes of her. Anger, again, and outrage.

'To make a *game*, a *wager*, a *bet*, with my *home*—' she broke off, overcome with emotion.

'But it isn't your home, is it? It has never been.' He looked at her consideringly. 'On the other hand...' he said, his manner still impassive and unconcerned, '...since all I'm going to do with it is sell it, because I've no use for it, I might be prepared to give you first refusal. If you can meet my price. Buy it back if you want. I've no objection.'

'And I...' she said tightly, '...have no money. All I have is the income from some money my father gave over to me when I turned eighteen, which allows me to live here frugally. But the capital isn't nearly enough to buy the *mas*. I told you, Naomi got everything when my father died.'

He let his eyes rest on her. 'Parents let you down,' he said. 'Never rely on them.' His voice had no expression. He gave a shrug and asked, 'So, no money?'

'Not nearly enough to buy back the *mas*,' she said.

'What will you do when you leave here?' he asked. As he did so, he wondered why he was asking. It was nothing to him.

'Go back to England,' she said.

'To do what?'

It was her turn to shrug. 'Get a job. Make a living. I don't know.'

'Well, before you leave, I'll want a tour of the house and whatever grounds there are. I'll want an inventory, too, of all the contents.' He poured himself another coffee and demolished the last croissant.

'Tell me, is there a pool? I haven't seen one.'

'It's at the gable end, not visible from here or your bedroom,' she answered. Her voice was hollow, as if she was doing her best to be disengaged.

'Good,' he nodded. 'I could do with a swim later in the afternoon.'

He drained his coffee. 'OK, let's start the tour.' He got to his feet. 'You can clear away later.'

He watched her stand up. She didn't say anything, but she didn't need to. It was all shown in her eyes—resentful, baleful, hostile.

And beautiful. Very, very beautiful...

He let his eyes rest on her. Her tee shirt did nothing for her except highlight the honeyed tan of her sun-kissed skin and her hair was now rigidly pulled back into some kind of tight knot on her head, but neither diminished her extraordinary beauty. A beauty she clearly did not flaunt and almost seemed oblivious to. She was completely different from the women he was used to. They were all chic, fashionable, immaculately groomed and keen to hang around wherever rich men gathered.

'What do you want to see first? House or grounds?' Her voice, interrupting his thoughts, was less hollow but still disengaged. As if feigning indifference. Or using it as protection....

But he did not care to think about what was motivating her, only that the interruption was welcome to him. His thoughts about women, the kind of women he'd become used to, were out of place here. Here, the only perfume came from the profusion of scented flowers. Not from bottles that cost a hundred euros or more.

'We're outdoors. Let's start here.' He said looking towards her expectantly. This beautiful woman who so openly resented his presence here and the reason for it. But what did he care about her resentment, or anything else about her? What did he even care about her beauty? It had no relevance to him. His only interest was in his latest acquisition. This *mas* in the middle of nowhere. He would inspect it, assess it and hand it over to the realtors to dispose of for the maximum profit.

'As you can see...' she started, unemotionally, this woman in whom he had no interest and who was only a source of currently useful information to him, '...the gardens are terraced. There are three levels leading down to the lavender fields. There's a gate at the bottom, so you can access the fields.'

'How many fields?' he asked. 'Do they come with the *mas*?'

'Just the two. Less than two hectares in all, but there is pasture land as well, and an olive grove and a citrus orchard. It's all rented to a neighbour, but not for money. It's done in return for keeping the trees pruned and so on. Payment is taken in produce—olive oil, meat, milk and cheese, lemons and oranges. The lavender goes to a perfumery near Grasse. The land was once far more extensive, but my grandmother sold a lot to try and reduce the debt on the property.'

'Why was there debt in the first place?'

'Farming is always uncertain. My great-grandfather, he was of the war generation and times were even harder during the Occupation, tried to make money in other ventures. They failed, hence the debts.'

She started to walk along the paved terrace, towards the far end of the house.

'This is where the pool is,' she said. 'My father had it installed.'

It wasn't a large pool, but it looked inviting, glinting azure in the sun. Padded loungers were set out between the water and the gable end of the house. A pair of white ducks were swimming happily across the water. An exclamation broke from her. The tone of her voice, speaking French, entirely different now. Indignant but affectionate. The contrast between the coolness with which she addressed him and the warmth with which she addressed the ducks could not have been more marked.

'Oh, Mathilde, Maurice! You know you should not swim here! You have your own pond! Shame on you!'

Lycos heard the clap of hands intended to shoo the ducks, who only quacked derisively in response and swam off defiantly in the opposite direction. A laugh broke from him, he couldn't help it.

'They know perfectly well they are not supposed to swim in the pool, but they just don't listen!' Arielle said indignantly, reverting to English. The animation in her voice was still audible.

'Let them,' he said. 'They're not doing any harm.' There was amused tolerance in his reply.

Her shoulders rose in a hapless shrug. 'Well, I don't suppose it's very hygienic, but they do so enjoy it and they know I indulge them. What's really irresistible is when they bring their ducklings here to learn to swim. They bob about adorably!'

The open warmth in her voice appealed to him.

'Have they got ducklings?' Lycos found himself asking. Why he should ask he did not know, but he did all the same.

She answered with a shake of her head.

'Not at the moment. Matilde usually lets Honore sit on her eggs when she lays a clutch.'

'Honore? Another duck?'

'No, she's one of the hens. They come into the garden, which helps with pest control, but they are mostly on the waste ground on the other side of the barn, by the pond. They get fed corn as well, for breakfast and in the evening. It's the only way to get them to come in and roost safely in the barn, or the foxes would make short work of them! The ducks come in then as well.'

He heard her voice change. Stiffen.

'Whatever...whatever happens to the *mas*, the poultry must go to my neighbours. They need to be looked after. If you consider them your property as well as everything else...' the twist in her voice was tight '...I will buy them off you.'

Lycos's eyes went back to the renegade ducks, splashing contentedly in the azure water, openly contemptuous of any attempt to get them to abandon this preferred location. They looked at home.

'There's no rush,' he heard himself say. Then, glancing around, he went on, 'OK, so what's next?'

She led the way past the pool, through a gateway in a high stone wall. He found himself at the front of the *mas*, beyond which was the gravelled space where he'd parked his car. The gateway leading into the cobbled courtyard was visible, along with the barns bordering the other side of the courtyard. Bordering the barns was open ground, in which the contours of a pond were visible. Presumably, he reckoned, the pond where the errant ducks should be. Hens were pecking haphazardly, and pigeons nestled on the tiled roof of the barns, their cooing soft and murmurous. It was very peaceful. The only thing that was out of place was his long, low car.

And himself.

'If you want to see the citrus orchard, it's beyond the pond,' she said, interrupting his surveillance of the scene.

Lycos shook his head. 'Later,' he said. 'First, show me the rest of the interior of the house.'

She led the way through into the cobbled courtyard and back into the kitchen, waiting while he looked about him.

The kitchen was large and old-fashioned, with a black range set in a fireplace. There was a slightly less old-fashioned electric stove, large old wooden store cupboards, a massive and solid-looking dresser with solid-looking earthenware crockery on its shelves, an ancient-looking refrigerator rumbling in a corner, an even more ancient-looking stone sink with wooden work surfaces either side. The centre of the room was dominated by a scrubbed oak table set with kitchen chairs. The combined scents of cinnamon, citrus and coffee from breakfast hung in the air.

He gave a nod and moved towards the door that led through to the central hallway and the parlour beyond. He'd seen the parlour already on his way out to the terrace earlier. As old-fashioned as everywhere else, the room was dominated by a large fireplace with a wood-burning stove and a handsome baby grand piano, which raised his eyebrows slightly though he said nothing. As he headed up the stairs, Arielle followed him.

'My room I know,' he said. 'Show me the other bedrooms.'

There were another three bedrooms. Two of them were small and just as old-fashioned as his own.

'The remaining bedroom is mine,' she said.

He glanced at her. 'Show me,' he said. It was not a request.

He saw her expression stiffen.

'Arielle,' he said, 'whatever your objections and protests and obvious resentment, this property does not belong to you. It belongs to me. So, show me the bedroom you have been using.'

For a moment, as they paused on the landing, her eyes refuted his assertion. Then, her gait as stiff as her expression, she opened the bedroom door. He stepped past her.

It was, very obviously, her bedroom. Just as old-fashioned as the others, but far more personal. Far more feminine. The walls were papered with pink roses, the pattern reflected in the quilt and the fabric covering the stool in front of the dressing table. An earthenware vase full of pink roses stood on the chest of drawers and the curtains were rose-patterned. The white painted chest of drawers also had a rose stencil adorning it, as did the large, old-fashioned wardrobe.

'Seen enough?' Her voice was cool. Hostile.

He gave a brief nod.

'You have an en-suite, or only the bathroom I used?'

With visible reluctance she opened a door that might have been to a dressing room, but was not. The bathroom was, predictably, old-fashioned. Whoever bought this place, Lycos opined, would have to gut it completely.

Well, that was their problem, not his. A realtor would probably seek to present it as a project or, even more optimistically, some kind of historic artefact.

'You hate it, don't you?'

Her voice was flat. His eyes suddenly met hers.

'My opinion is irrelevant,' he said. 'All that matters to me is that it is sold for the best price it can achieve. I have no other interest.'

He turned and walked out of the room, heading downstairs again. Something about her accusation, for an accusation it was, riled him. He glanced at his watch. It was nearing midday. He should collect his suitcase, get into his car and head off. Make for Paris. Select a realtor. Get the paperwork of possession sorted and then hand this place over for sale.

She'll have to be evicted.

Would she go quietly? With or without her livestock? Which probably wasn't hers anyway, any more than the *mas* was. He frowned a moment. He would need to carefully check that she had no legal claim on the property. She'd said she'd tried to make a claim and had failed, but maybe she'd just lacked a decent lawyer. Well, he could afford the best lawyers and they would ascertain his own claim. And if there was any doubt about it, then Gerald Maitland would pay the price for it. Staking what was not his to stake was unforgiveable when playing the Wolf....

'Are you going now?'

Arielle's voice from the top of the stairs made him turn. It had been coolly spoken and he could see her hand gripping the banister. She obviously wanted him to go. To leave her here. Enjoy what little time was left to her in the place she was so clearly reluctant to accept was never hers in the first place.

'No,' he said.

Instantly, he frowned. Why the hell had he just said that? He'd been on the point of leaving, but now—

'I'll stay the night,' he announced.

Arielle's grip on the banister tightened. Then, stepping downstairs, she asked in a constricted voice, 'Why?'

The dark, unreadable eyes rested on her. 'I don't believe...' Lycos Dimistrios said, '...that that is any of your business. As I have repeatedly said, I am the new owner of this property and what I want will be.'

Her chin went up. 'I only have your word that you have acquired it from my stepbrother!'

His answer was a shrug. 'I have it in writing. And if that doesn't suffice, contact him. He'll confirm it. He'll have no choice.'

Arielle's face contorted. 'I wouldn't speak to that toad if he were on his deathbed!'

Another shrug came her way. 'Then don't contact him. It's no concern of mine.' She watched him make his way into the parlour, settle himself into an armchair and get out his phone, paying no more attention to her. For a moment or two she just stood there, fulminating, until she heard him start to speak in French. He was speaking to someone called Marc and was saying he had been delayed and wanted to rearrange his meeting. She left him to it and stalked into the kitchen. Her thoughts were full. Beyond full.

The implications of what had happened this morning were overwhelming her and out of nowhere she felt her heart start to race and pound. She leant against the stone sink, trying to get control of herself, but it was impossible. She felt herself start to shake. More than shake—convulse. A cry broke from her, tore her throat and dry sobs racked her body.

It had happened. It had finally, finally happened. The sword that had been hanging over her head since the day she'd read her father's will, since she'd heard Naomi's hateful voice and Gerald's even more hateful one mocking her and taking from her all that she held most dear, had finally fallen. Finally sliced her through...

'Arielle?'

She didn't hear her name being spoken. Her eyes were screwed shut and the uncontrollable shaking of her body would not stop, nor would the dry, cracking sobs in her throat.

'Arielle—stop. This is hysteria.'

She felt her hands seized and pressed together in a much stronger grip than hers, so tightly it distracted her. She flung open her eyes. Lycos Dimistrios, who had arrived like a marauding pirate to take everything from her, was there right in front of her. His expression was strange. Concerned.

'I said stop,' he said again. 'Get control of yourself. Control is essential. Without it you are nothing. No one. Without control you are vulnerable. A victim.'

His eyes were holding hers, like hooks, not letting them go. The force in them was impossible to deny. Impossible to defy...

With racking breaths, she heard her dry, cracking sobs start to die away and her convulsions finally ceased.

He nodded curtly.

'That's better.' He let go of her hands as he reached

past her, taking an upturned glass from the draining board and filling it with cold water from the tap over the sink.

'Drink this,' he said. 'All of it.'

She did, though she had to force it past her constricted throat. He stepped back while she drank, but his eyes never left her face.

'Better?' he asked, as she carefully replaced the glass.

She blinked. Her heart rate was returning to normal, her breathing easing.

'Yes,' she said faintly. She made to turn away, but a hand closed around her upper arm.

'Sit down,' he said. He guided her to one of the kitchen chairs, lowered her down on it and she sat unresistingly. He sat himself down as well and looked across the table at her.

'We had better talk,' he said.

For a moment Lycos said nothing, collecting his thoughts. It had been...unnerving...to witness something that had all the hallmarks of a hysterical collapse. Her complete, uncontrollable, uncontrolled breakdown in front of his eyes. His thoughts now were conflicted. He'd sat her down and said they had better talk, but he didn't want to. Why should he? It was nothing to him that she was upset because she was nothing to him. Yet, all the same, he took a breath.

As he looked across at her he saw that her face was blank. Not with the resistance she'd presented so far, but with a kind of emptiness.

'Arielle, you've had a shock. Something bad you've been holding at bay has finally happened. Now you're having to deal with it. But look at it this way. You've known since your father died, so you told me, that you are going to have to relinquish what you'd expected to inherit. There's nothing you can do about it. Accept it. You don't have a choice and you know...'

Something edged into his voice he didn't want to think about.

'...when you have no choice, it...it frees you. That might sound illogical, but it isn't. You don't have to fight any more. You don't have to fear any more. The worst has happened. That's it.'

He fell silent, eyes masking a moment. Then he spoke again. Slowly this time.

'When the worst has happened, nothing more can hurt you. That's a kind of freedom you know. It has...a value. When choice is taken from you, so is responsibility. Do you understand what I'm telling you?'

Her face was still blank. He went on. He didn't want to think about where his words were coming from.

Didn't want to remember.

'You've felt responsible, haven't you? For this place. You told me it's been in your mother's family for generations. Now it's gone. It isn't your fault that it's gone. If there was any fault it was, if you think about it, your mother's fault in trusting your father. And before that it was your great-grandfather's fault for putting debt on it. So, because it's not your fault it's gone, it's not your responsibility either.'

He could see her face work now, her hands clenching.

'But I don't want it gone,' she said in a faint voice.

He gave a sigh. 'The secret of a happy life, Arielle...'

he said in a very dry tone, '...is only to want what we can get.' He took another breath. 'If you want this place then my advice to you is this. Go back to England and make some money, enough to make whoever buys this place an offer they won't want to refuse.'

She looked at him. 'I don't know how to make money.'

'Then learn!' he said impatiently. 'Anyone can do it! I'm proof of that—'

He broke off suddenly and stood up. 'That's enough of a life lesson for now. I'm hungry. What's for lunch?'

It was a distraction, he knew, but it was also what he happened to want right then.

And getting what he wanted, whatever it was, was the most compelling life lesson that he had learnt. And lived by.

Arielle's voice interrupted his familiar mantra, sounding hesitant, 'I usually just have salad for lunch.'

'What kind?'

She replied, still sounding hesitant, 'Tomatoes, peppers, lettuce, cheese and ham. That sort of thing.'

Lycos nodded. 'Sounds good. Let's eat outside.'

She was still hesitant, so he crossed to the ancient looking fridge, which was rumbling to itself in the corner, and opened it. He brought out what he could find by way of cheese, ham and butter, and put it all on the table. He knew that some of the baguette he'd brought with him remained from their breakfast. Arielle collected herself sufficiently to fetch tomatoes and a gold-yellow pepper from a large bowl by the sink.

'I'll... I'll go and cut some lettuce,' he heard her say as she headed outside. Lycos let her be. She needed to come down completely from that state of mental turmoil she'd succumbed to. He busied himself loading up the wooden breakfast tray, wondering when he'd last had to prepare his own lunch. Arielle returned with a handful of leaves, washing them and then tossing them in a crockery bowl with oil and vinegar. She didn't speak and neither did Lycos. He picked up the tray.

'Ready?' he asked and made his way out to the terrace. The midday heat hit him and he was glad of the shady awning. Arielle emerged with the salad bowl, a jug of water and two glasses. Lycos sat himself down, as did she, and he started to help himself to bread, cheese and ham, and a couple of the ripe tomatoes. He got stuck in.

'This is good cheese,' he said.

'My neighbour makes it,' Arielle said. 'The ham is from their pigs too.' Her voice was back to sounding studiedly neutral.

She poured water into the glasses. Lycos took a draught, wondering when he'd last drank tap water, and only that, during a meal. But it was cold and refreshing with a distinct taste to it, unlike city water, and he remarked as such.

'It's from the original well,' Arielle said. 'Though it's pumped up by electricity now, not by hand.' She paused and he could see she wanted to say something else. Then she did.

'When...when you said what you said about responsibility...did you mean that?'

'Yes,' he said, looking across at her. 'You can let this place go, Arielle, because nothing about it or what's happened to it, is your responsibility. Except, maybe...' he allowed a trace of rare humour to creep into his voice, '...for your poultry. You can find new homes for them with my blessing. Though...' he added '...I suspect unless Matilde and Maurice get a swimming pool of their own, wherever they end up they won't be best pleased!'

She gave a wry, if reluctant, laugh. Lycos liked the sound of it. He let his gaze rest on her for a moment from beneath his lashes. He wanted, he realised, for her to get over what was obviously a blow to her. Discovering that what she'd said she'd been dreading, her stepbrother disposing of the *mas*, had actually happened. Get over it and...

And what?

His gaze rested on her a moment longer. She really was, he knew, exceptionally lovely.

Maybe, now he was here, he should take advantage of that.

Thoughts flickered in his head. Yes, he was here, but he wasn't exactly going to stay, was he?

Her hesitant voice interrupted his thoughts.

'When are you planning to sell?' she asked. Her voice was low and she didn't look at him.

'I'll be putting it on the market when I get to Paris. I was on my way there, driving up from the coast, when I decided to stop off and take a look this morning.'

'Do you live in Paris?'

'I don't live anywhere. I stay in hotels or rent apartments if I'm anywhere for any duration.'

'But you're based in Greece?' she sounded puzzled, making an assertion she seemed to assume must be the case.

'That's the last place I'd call home.'

He hadn't intended there to be an edge in his voice, but it was there all the same.

'Why?'

She was looking at him now, straight at him, with those celestial blue eyes of hers. As if she could see into him. Or wanted to.

'Why?' he echoed. 'Because... I escaped.'

'From what?'

He drew back, dropping his knife on the table. 'What is this? Psychoanalysis?'

'Not really. But you've seen fit to lecture me about my circumstances. I... I'm simply retaliating.'

He gave a laugh. A short one, but a laugh for all that. Although there was an edge to it too.

'From things I wanted to escape from. Mainly poverty. And I have. Now I can get things I want. That's why, Arielle, I say the same to you. If you make money, you can get what you want.'

The blue eyes were still looking at him. 'How did you?' she asked. 'Escape poverty?'

'I discovered I had a skill and I honed it, until I could use it on others. On people with money. To remove it from them—or enough of it to enrich me in the end.'

She frowned. 'What skill?'

'I told you already. The same way I acquired this place. I gamble, Arielle. That's my skill.' He met her frowning gaze.

'So you are a professional gambler? Is that it, you make a living out of gambling?

He shook his head. That was easy to answer too.

'No, I make a living out of investing the money I make out of gambling. Gambling provided me with capital, lump sums, that I then could invest in whatever it is in the world that makes money. Once you have money, Arielle, it's easy enough to make more. Millionaires and billionaires don't have to work hard to stay rich. The markets do it for them. Providing they stay sensible, they'll make more money. Or, rather, they themselves won't. Their fund managers will make it for them and cream off a percentage from their clients to make their money while they're at it.'

'But you do still gamble? You just won the *Mas Delfine* off my stepbrother by gambling.'

He could hear the bitterness that the place she loved had changed hands in a game of cards in her voice, but he ignored it.

'To keep my hand in,' he said. 'To pay, if you like, homage to the skill that made me rich. We should not, Arielle, neglect our roots.' His voice was dry and self-mocking, yet cautionary. He would never, must never, forget his roots. His origins. Or he might become like the other rich idiots out there who took their wealth for granted.

He wanted to change the subject away from himself. He was not used to talking about himself—he never did. He was no one's business but his own.

'So,' he said his voice changing as he helped himself to another sweet tomato. 'What's your skill, Arielle? Besides looking after this place and attempting to shoo ducks off the swimming pool?' He let humour lighten his voice, as his eyes went to her questioningly. 'With luck it might be a skill you could use to make enough money to buy this place back.'

She gave a rueful half-smile. 'My skill isn't one that yields much likelihood of riches,' she told him.

'What is it?' Lycos asked.

'Music. I studied it. Went to music college. But there is a huge number of good musicians out there and only a few make a living. Even fewer make a good living and almost none become virtuosos or stars! My mother always encouraged me though and my father was happy enough to pay for my studies. He gave me the piano in the parlour, so I have that to thank him for. Then…' Arielle hesitated as a shadow moved over her face, '…after I'd graduated my mother became ill, so I came here to look after her. I stayed with her until she died. Then I stayed on, while I mourned her and then… Well, my father remarried four months later.'

She continued, 'And because I loathed Naomi, and because she wanted only my obliteration and non-existence, I stayed here until my father died within a year of marrying Naomi and… Well, you know the rest. So, here I am. Until…' she said with resignation, or maybe even acceptance he thought, '…you throw me out.'

She'd cleared her plate too and she got to her feet, packing away the dishes back on the tray. Lycos did not help her. He only watched her deft, quick movements. Thoughts were moving inside his head and he was not sure what to make of them. The heat of the day was palpable, even there shaded below the awning. All around, cicadas sang their constant chorus, while birdsong interrupted as if an occasional vocalist. The air was somnolent with fragrance from the honeysuckle winding over a nearby pergola and the lavender lining the stone walls. The heat radiated up from the stone paving of the terrace.

Arielle disappeared indoors with her laden tray. Lycos stretched out his legs, lounged back in his chair and let his gaze rest on the gardens beyond the terrace. His mood was strange. This whole place was strange. Alien to his life.

His life was nothing like this place. This time yesterday he'd been doing a tough workout in the gym at his hotel on the Côte d'Azur, knowing he was heading for the casino that evening to, as he had just told Arielle, keep his hand in. And at that moment, he should be checked into his hotel in Paris, where he should be meeting Marc Derenz of *Banc Derenz* for dinner at one of the city's Michelin-starred restaurants. The next morning in his formal review being shown spreadsheets, graphs and forecasts, making decisions, moving money and investments around. Checking out an appropriate realtor to discuss the best price he could get for this latest acquisition. This remote, old-fashioned Provençal *mas* in the middle of nowhere, with its hens and a pair of over-indulged ducks, and its very own version of Cinderella with a wicked stepmother and decidedly ugly and brutish stepsibling…

And shall I be her Prince Charming?

Charming her into his bed…?

He felt the question take shape in his head. Wondering, considering, how to answer it. He wasn't yet sure. But there was no rush, after all, to answer it. He wasn't going anywhere for now. And that, he realised as he flexed his outstretched legs, recrossed his ankles and lounged back in his seat, felt strangely good...

CHAPTER FOUR

ARIELLE FINISHED THE washing up and wondered what to do next. Her mind was still blank. A strange air of dissociation seemed to be possessing her. A kind of preternatural calm. Maybe it was some kind of aftershock. She stared blankly out of the kitchen window recalling her juddering reaction earlier when she'd been totally overwhelmed. She had very nearly gone into a complete breakdown, shaking and convulsing like that, terrifyingly out of control...

But he stopped it—pulled me back.

His blunt words came back to her—that her home had never been hers in the first place. Protest rose in her throat, then subsided. Bleakness filled her.

I have to face the truth. That Mas Delphine *was never mine. So it was never mine to lose.*

Pulling that self-protective sense of dissociation around her as best she could, she went out onto the terrace. There was no sign of the man. She could not see him anywhere in the gardens, nor by the pool when she walked past it. Yet his monstrous car was still there, parked in the shade of the old chestnut tree by the pond. Suddenly she could feel the oppressive heat and an immense sense of weariness overcoming her. Exhaustion of mind, body and spirit from the catastrophe that had broken over her like a pitiless tsunami that morning. She felt herself sink down onto one of the padded loungers, shaded by the house. She leant back on it shutting her eyes. She would rest. Just for a moment...

Lycos lifted his head from his pillow, for a second not knowing where he was. Then recall flooded through him. He was at the *mas* he'd won from the boorish Gerald Maitland. He'd diverted off the road to Paris to take a look at it. He rose to his feet, feeling refreshed. He'd gone up to the bedroom as the effect of driving all night had caught up with him and had flaked out on the counterpane. He glanced at his watch. He must have slept for a good couple of hours and the light had changed in the dusky room. Crossing to the window he looked out over the garden and the view beyond. He'd made the decision to stay the night. But why?

There was nothing to keep him here. He'd seen the place, got the measure of it, knew what to instruct whatever realtor he engaged to sell it for him. So, there was no point in staying longer. He might as well return to his normal life.

And yet...

His gaze rested on the scene beyond. It really was lovely and very peaceful. Nothing was moving, other than a few hens who'd wandered into the garden and were pecking about in the vegetation, and the chorus of cicadas was soothing. The scent of honeysuckle and lavender wafted up to him, fragrant in the warm air. He flexed his shoulders. A swim would be good. If the ducks had no objection.

His mouth tugged into a half-smile unconsciously as he turned away. He put his suitcase onto the bed, lifting layers till he'd found his swim shorts. He swiftly changed into them keeping his polo shirt on. He collected his sunglasses and helped himself to the bath towel from his shower that morning, which had been drying on an old-fashioned wooden towel rack beside the wardrobe. Barefoot, he headed downstairs, let himself out onto the terrace and made his way around to the pool. Where Arielle was he had no idea, but right now his focus was on the pool.

He turned the corner of the house and stopped dead. He'd found not Cinderella, but Sleeping Beauty fast asleep on a lounger in the shade.

Slowly, silently, on bare feet on the paving stones, he went up to her and gazed down at her. She was half on her side, the yellow tee shirt pulled across her breasts, outlining them and shaping them for his view. Her slender legs were slanted, bare arms by her sides. Her hair was coming loose from its confining knot, forming tendrils around her face. He could see her breathe softly, her breasts rising and falling gently, her eyelashes dusky on the tender curve of her cheek, her lips very slightly parted.

Of its own volition his hand reached out, one finger carefully brushing away a lock of hair that was teasing the corner of her mouth. Did she sense his touch, light though it had been? She moved slightly and he drew his hand back, but continued to gaze down at her. She really was so very, very lovely.

Like no other woman I've seen...

The women he usually consorted with were a world away from this pastoral Sleeping Beauty. His women, the ones he selected for his pleasure when pleasure was what he wanted, were chic and sophisticated. They had perfect hair, perfect make-up, perfect sex appeal and perfect allure. All carefully, deliberately, prepared for his delectation. They knew exactly what a man like him wanted and provided it for him. Trophy women. Groomed to within an inch of their pampered lives to adorn the arm of a rich man and share a little of his riches, while it pleased him to permit them to do so.

Nothing, nothing at all like the Sleeping Beauty now lying there for him in all her natural loveliness.

Not even knowing that he was looking at her.

How long he stood—motionless, gazing down at her—he didn't know. All that he knew was that thoughts were moving inside him. More than thoughts. He wanted to reach out his hand again, touch her, stroke the soft curve of her cheek, trace the parted outline of her lips, lean down towards her...brush her mouth with his. Taste the sweetness that she promised. Taste all of it. Taste all of her...

Resolve shaped itself in him. He had not expected to come into possession of this farmhouse in the middle of Provence. He had not expected to follow an impulse to find it, inspect it and assess it. He had not expected to find it occupied by this pastoral Sleeping Beauty, this hard-done-by Cinderella.

And yet, so it was. And because it was, he would pause

a while. Take his time here, in this quiet, peaceful, unexpected place, and enjoy what it had to offer. Enjoy all of it.

His gaze lingered on Arielle, so peacefully asleep.

And she can enjoy it too. I can be her Prince Charming. Charm her away from her woes for a while. Divert her from her unhappiness at losing her home.

He stepped away, moving to the other lounger, dropping his towel and sunglasses down on it. He shrugged off his polo shirt and walked to the edge of the pool. The trespassing ducks had vanished. He thought he could see two white forms under some bushes on the far side of the pool with their heads tucked under their wings, sleeping. Bracing his body at the edge of the pool, he swallow-dived into its cooling depths, disappearing beneath the water into the world beneath.

Behind him, on the shaded lounger, Arielle's eyes flew open.

She started. What had woken her? She propped herself up on her elbow, eyes widened. Then she realised what had roused her. In the pristine waters of the azure pool the lithe, masculine form of the man who was taking her home from her, ploughed down the length in a strong crawl. He reached the end swiftly, turned and returned down the length, repeating the process several times as she simply stared.

Words rang hollow in her head.

Well, it's his pool now, along with every other centimetre of my home.

The bitter truth was hard to swallow. Impossible to accept. Yet accept it she must.

Stiffly, she got to her feet. She would leave him to it. Taking possession of her swimming pool, making himself at home in it. Just as he was making himself at home in the entire place and ousting her from all that she loved so much.

He reached the end of the pool again, pausing this time. He looked across at her with one forearm thrown across the tiled edge to hold him in place in the deep water. His dark hair was sleek on his head, lashes loaded with water, cheekbones glistening.

'Care to join me?' he asked.

Arielle shook her head.

'Why not?' he challenged.

She only shook her head again. She knew she ought to move away, leave him to it, but something held her back. Something kept her eyes fixated on him, unable to look away. He was good-looking, lethally so. She'd known that from the moment he'd strolled into the courtyard in the early morning sunshine with his dress tie loose, the top button of his dress shirt undone and as rough jawed as he had been. As if he were a pirate who had come to seize all she possessed and held dear.

She'd known it again when he'd come down to lunch, freshly-shaven. With his night-dark eyes, his chiselled cheekbones, his bladed nose and the sensual curve of his mouth. Wearing his expensively-styled casual wear, seeming more at home on the glitzy Riviera than at an old-fashioned Provençal *mas*.

And there in that moment, she knew it all over again as her eyes looked over his broad, bare shoulders, his half-exposed, leanly muscled torso, his bared forearm, his sleek, slick wet hair and his diamond-laden lashes.

She knew it. She felt it.

Felt the strange hollowing inside her that had nothing, absolutely nothing, to do with all the tumult and aftershock of what this day had brought her. What this man had done to her.

She turned away, her face burning suddenly with a heat that had not come from the late afternoon sun. She turned and hurried away.

Hearing, as if an echo, a soft laugh behind her...

Lycos dipped below the water again. His soft laugh silenced, but the reason for it still resonant within him, as he dolphin-kicked the length of the pool before surfacing. A sense of satisfaction filled him. He knew why she had refused and he was glad of it. He had seen the sudden flush in her cheeks as she'd turned away.

He slowed his stroke, easing back to a more leisurely, steady pace. Lapping the lengths and pondering as he did so. Any of his other women, the ones he was used to, would have instantly either accepted his invitation, eager to respond, or else would have turned it down coquettishly, flirtatiously.

Arielle had simply blushed.

And walked away.

As his pace slowed, he thought about it. Found words shaping themselves in his head. Unfamiliar words.

All I have seen from her, all day, is emotion. Shock, dismay, distress. So much emotion. Raw and uncontrolled. I have seen her as she is. Nothing hidden.

It was a strange realisation. An unfamiliar one. What did he know of any of the women he'd consorted with? They'd always put forward a persona, an image, a facsimile of whoever they were. He'd never penetrated behind that persona. Never questioned who they really were, if they were anyone at all, whether they had any existence other than the one he required them to have.

But I keep myself from them, too. I keep myself from everyone.

He knew why he did that. There'd been too much in the past for anything else. Too much that he didn't want to think about, to remember. It was the way he operated. The way that worked for him. The way he had become over the long years that separated him from the past. The way he was familiar with.

He knew no other way to be. No other way he wanted to be.

As he reached the shallow end of the pool he halted abruptly. He waded out of the pool using the corner steps, feeling the warmth of the late afternoon sun on his bare shoulders. He strode to his lounger, seized the towel to pad himself dry, then, looping it around his neck, slid on his sunglasses, scooped up his polo shirt and headed back indoors.

From the cool hallway he could hear clattering coming from the kitchen and caught the aroma of garlic. He paused by the door, leaning against the jamb.

'Dinner?' he queried.

Arielle was by the sink, chopping onions on a wooden board.

'*Boeuf bourguignon,*' she said. She did not look at him. 'It will take a good hour.'

'No problem,' Lycos returned easily. 'I'm going up to shower and change. An aperitif would be good when I come down. Enjoy it with me.'

He didn't bother to wait for an answer. He simply vaulted lightly up the stairs and disappeared into the bathroom, removing his dark glasses as he did.

The swim had done him good. Or something had.

In a pleasant mood he stepped inside the shower cubicle and turned on the water.

Arielle chopped the onion into smaller pieces more vigorously than was necessary. Her lips were tightened. Inside her chest she could feel her heart beating and she knew why. But she paid it no attention and instead, she focussed on cooking. She knew the reason for that too...

Onions chopped to within an inch of their life, she extracted beef steaks from the freezer. She cubed them and then tossed them in seasoned flour, then seared them. She then added the steak to the iron pan, along with the chopped garlic, onions and a plentiful amount of fresh thyme from the pots in the garden. She poured in a good measure of wine and set it all to simmer. Would her uninvited and unwelcome guest require a dessert as well? Her mouth tightened further at the thought, for Lycos Dimistrios was no more her 'guest' than Genghis Khan had been a 'guest' of those receiving his grim visitation.

For a moment she felt an overwhelming urge to march upstairs and bawl him out. Yell at him for being demanding, entitled and obnoxious. Then she sighed. What would that get her? An order to pack her bags and get out. She took a breath to steady herself.

Stick it out this evening. He'll leave in the morning and then, until he formally sells and evicts you, you can at least stay here. It could be weeks before a buyer wants the place. Precious weeks for you...

For that reason, and that reason alone, she would put up with his overbearing behaviour. And certainly not because he could raise her pulse in ways that had absolutely nothing to do with the reason he was here. She crushed that wayward, illicit and completely irrelevant-to-the-dire-situation thought way down.

What does it matter what he looks like? It's who he is. He's the man who won my home in a stupid, vile game of cards! So, I should totally ignore anything else about him.

She picked up a metal sieve and headed out for the walled section of the gardens that had been set aside as a kitchen garden. She would pick raspberries, soak them in liqueur and serve them with ice cream from the freezer.

Back in the kitchen she rinsed the raspberries and left them to drain. She then topped and tailed the beans she'd also picked to go with the beef and stirred the aromatic *bourguignon* simmering gently in its heavy iron pan on the hob. She felt hot and sticky from the day's heat and from the cooking. She usually swam this time of day...

Well, why not? He's had his swim. I can have mine. In his pool?

Defiantly, damning him for everything he was, she headed upstairs. A moment later she ran back down again, tee shirt over her costume and towel in her hand, and made for the cooling waters of the pool.

* * *

Lycos was strolling in the gardens. He'd intended to fetch his laptop from the boot of his car, but as he'd headed outdoors, refreshed after his shower, the early evening air had drawn him into the gardens instead. He stepped down to the lower levels of terracing, inhaled the heady scent of lavender and watched the sun lowering behind the trees. From far away he thought he could hear cattle lowing and the faint, plaintive bleat of sheep. As he made his way back up to the top level, he realised he could hear the sound of water lapping. Curious, he glanced through to the pool area.

Arielle was swimming. Not as he had swum, with vigorous freestyle, but with a slow and graceful breaststroke. Her head was up out of the water with her hair piled up on top. All he could see of her was her shoulders and the dim outline of her body beneath the surface. He watched her for a moment as she headed away from him, unaware of his observation, and then he let her be as he went back to exploring the grounds of his new possession.

Returning via the courtyard, he entered the house by the kitchen door, drawn by the appetising aroma of the dinner cooking. He picked up the long wooden spoon resting on a plate and lifted the heavy lid of the iron pan, starting to stir the contents.

'What are you doing?'

The voice from the doorway was sharp.

He looked round, unperturbed. Arielle stood there in the doorframe, glaring at him.

'Giving it a stir,' he said.

'It's fine,' came the retort.

His eyes went to her. She had a towel wrapped around her, and was dripping on the tiled kitchen floor.

'It smells good,' he said.

'I'm glad you approve.'

Lycos ignored the sardonic note. 'When you've showered and dressed you can share that aperitif with me,' he said.

'I've got to feed the hens first and lock them up. And the ducks,' she retorted.

'Well, when you've done that you can share that aperitif with me,' Lycos amended. 'I'll give you a hand with the poultry. Mathilde and Maurice may not come quietly,' he added, with a twist of humour.

'No, they come with a lot of quacking and a great deal of expectation of being fed as well as locked up for the night!'

Lycos's eyes glinted. 'You see, you can do humour too, if you put your mind to it,' he said.

Immediately, her expression tightened. Saying nothing, she walked past him and a moment later he heard her padding up the stairs. He went back to stirring the *bourguignon*. He should not have teased her, it had been unkind of him.

Today has not been good for her.

He set aside the wooden spoon, replaced the heavy lid and walked to the kitchen door. The daylight was definitely fading now and evening was starting to gather. So, he realised with a sudden tug at his mouth, were the hens. He could see several pecking about near the gateway, clearly knowing it was their suppertime. One particularly bold, or hungry, hen headed towards him making a clucking noise.

'Not me, *madame*,' he said apologetically. He watched a while as, unwilling to believe he did not have her feed about his person, the hen pecked near his feet, at what he did not know. Upstairs he heard the sound of shower water. Then, moments later, it cut out. He leant against the doorframe, relaxing against it. It really was very peaceful here, the evening air soft and warm. His eyes went to his car, visible through the open gateway. It seemed quite out of place.

A peck at his feet distracted him. He glanced down. The hen had clearly not believed him.

'*Madame*,' he informed her apologetically. 'That is my shoe, not your dinner!'

A voice behind him spoke. 'That's Hortense—she's always first in the line.'

Arielle was coming into the kitchen, dressed now. She'd put on long cotton trousers and a light, but long-sleeved sweatshirt, both in blue. The colour matched her eyes, Lycos noted absently, making them look even bluer. Even more beautiful.

'Their feed is kept in the barn,' she said.

Lycos watched her head across the courtyard, opening the feedstore door and emerging with a metal bowl filled with corn. Immediately she was surrounded by the entire flock of hens, clucking loudly. She led them into the henhouse, their wings flapping eagerly. Moments later she backed out, shutting them in and locking the door with a lowered bar. Then she turned around.

'Time for Maurice and Mathilde,' she announced,

heading back into the grain store to emerge again with the refilled bowl. A noisy quacking filled the air and suddenly Maurice and Mathilde were bustling forward from the direction of the pool, necks outstretched.

'They sleep next door to the hens,' Arielle said and led them into the duck-house, repeating the procedure as with the hens.

'All done,' she said, replacing the now empty bowl back in the grain store.

'My turn next,' said Lycos. 'For feeding. After...' he added purposefully, '...that aperitif. What does your sommelier recommend?' he quizzed.

'*Vin d'hôtes*,' came the tart reply. 'From my neighbour's vineyard.'

'*Ça suffit bien*,' Lycos murmured, standing aside so she could get into the kitchen. He watched while she extracted two wine glasses and then fetched a bottle of wine from a wooden rack. She took the glasses and handed the bottle to him, along with an ancient, and very primitive, corkscrew.

'You can watch the sun set over your new domain,' she said, leaving him to follow her across the hallway, then out on to the terrace.

He heard the sudden choke in her voice. Saw, as he came out on to the terrace, her shoulders hunch as she put the glasses on the ironwork table. He set the bottle and corkscrew down beside the glasses. Lifted his hand to her hunched shoulder.

'Arielle—'

He said her name, his voice low, felt her flinch beneath his touch. Something moved in him, but he did not know what. Only that it was not what he usually felt about another human being.

Or himself.

She pulled away, reached for the corkscrew, seized the bottle and begun ferociously busying herself with opening it before placing it back on the table.

'Your aperitif, *m'sieu*,' she said. Her chin was lifted. Defying the crack in her defences.

'Thank you,' he told her gravely. 'But you must share it with me. I insist.'

He held her chair for her and, stiffly, she sat down. He took his own place. He reached for the bottle, pouring equal measures into both glasses. The setting sun streamed golden light over the gardens. The cicadas were insistent in their chorus. Lycos watched her shakily lift her glass and he lifted his in unison. He looked across the table at her and held her gaze with his own.

'To survival, Arielle. Whatever the blows that fall.' He paused. Kept his gaze steady on her. 'You will survive them all, if you find the strength to do so.' He saw the uncertainty in her eyes. The doubt. The fear.

'Believe me,' he said. 'I know.'

Arielle lifted her fork, making a start on the *bourguignon*. An air of unreality possessed her. It was the strangest meal. Here she was sharing dinner and conversing civilly, if stiffly, with a man whose existence she had been completely unaware of not even twenty-four hours previously. A man who was creating a conflict within her that she could make no sense of. None at all. Because the only thing that made any sense to her, the only thing thundering in her head, was that this complete stranger was taking her beloved home away from her.

Yet he was having an effect on her that she could deplore all she liked, try to ignore all she liked, that had nothing to do with that nightmare. Nothing at all...

She felt her gaze fix on him. His face was lit by the soft light from the table lamp, that she'd switched on as the last of the daylight had faded with the setting sun, throwing his chiselled features into relief and yet somehow reflecting in the dark of his eyes, flecking them with gold. She felt something catch inside her. A tiny, silent gulp. A slight, sudden breathlessness. She wanted to shift her gaze, but couldn't. It seemed to be stuck. The sense of sudden breathlessness intensified.

With distinct effort she dragged her gaze away, dropping her eyes to her plate, taking another mouthful of food. She became aware that Lycos, having already drained his glass of wine, was reaching for the bottle. He glanced in her direction.

'This is surprisingly good,' he said. 'May I top you up?'

Arielle nodded absently, hoping he hadn't noticed her gazing at him.

'Perhaps I should call on your neighbours and introduce myself,' he said as he lifted his refilled glass to his mouth.

Arielle stared. 'What for? I'll tell them what's happened. I'll tell them to watch out for realtors descending and an eventual sale.'

'It would be more civil if I did that,' he countered, resuming his eating.

She continued to stare at him. 'Why would you want to be civil? You've only turned up here to check out your latest gambling win, which you've now done. So tomorrow you can head on to Paris.'

She could hear the tightness in her own voice and she reached for her glass, suddenly wanting the strength that came from wine. In the lamplight she could see a considering look cross Lycos's face.

'I might stay another day,' he said.

Arielle set her glass down with a click on the ironwork table.

'Why?' she demanded. She didn't want him hanging around. She wanted him gone. Gone, gone, gone. So she could mourn in private.

Have this last...this very last, time here.

Anguish clutched at her, and she could not stop it. Dimly, she was aware Lycos was replying.

'It's very pleasant here,' he was saying, but she noticed that there was something new in his voice. Something she hadn't heard before. She looked at him again and saw a musing expression in his lamp-lit face. He lifted a hand and gestured around.

'Relaxing,' he said. 'Just sitting here, dining *en plein air*, like this, with the warmth all around and the cicadas and no traffic noise. No noise at all,' he mused. His face tilted up.

'And the stars above,' he said. He lowered his hand so that it covered the table lamp, bringing the heavens instantly to light. 'Looks like that van Gogh painting,' he remarked. 'Starry, starry night...'

Arielle's face tightened. She didn't want Lycos Dimistrios saying things like that, she didn't want him praising the *Mas Delfine*, or the wine or anything else. She didn't want him full stop. His gaze dropped to her. A sardonic tug pulled at his mouth.

'Why don't you just hold up a sign saying, "Go Away",' he said cynically.

She didn't answer, only attacked her *boeuf bourguignon* with renewed force. A low laugh broke from him and he picked up his own fork again. After a moment he spoke.

'I mean it, Arielle, I might stay another day. There's no rush for me to reach Paris. And, like I said, this really is very pleasant. Good food and drink, a warm evening, a starry sky, the scent of...' He paused, looking at her quizzically.

'Jasmine,' she said shortly. 'It's always more fragrant at night.'

'Jasmine,' he echoed meditatively. He set down his fork, plate cleared. 'That was good,' he said approvingly. 'Maybe, I should keep you on as my personal chef while I'm here,' he said with the sardonic note back in his voice, although it was tinged with something else. 'Tell me, what is for dessert? And what liqueurs might there be? The evening calls for something sweet, I feel, on both counts.'

Saying nothing, Arielle stood up, cleared the plates and marched indoors. She didn't want his compliments, or his praise, or anything at all. She felt her eyes sting as she went into the kitchen, and she blinked rapidly. She didn't want him here at all.

But there was nothing, absolutely nothing, that she could do about it.

A hand squeezed around her heart, hard and painful. And despairing.

* * *

Lycos stretched out his legs under the table, switched off the table lamp and lifted his face to the stars as the rich wine coursed through his veins, replete from that very good *boeuf bourguignon*.

Relaxed.

He frowned slightly, gazing upwards at the stars studding the night sky. They burned much more vividly here than they ever did at the coast with all the light pollution from buildings and lit up yachts. Other than the cicadas he really couldn't hear a thing, maybe just vague sounds coming from the direction of the kitchen.

When had he last felt this relaxed? It was a pointless question because the answer was that he never felt relaxed. Not like this.

He heard Arielle emerge from the house and reaching out a hand he flicked the table lamp back on. She deposited a tray on the table holding dessert—a carton of vanilla ice cream and a bowl of raspberries—along with a square glass bottle and two small glasses.

'That looks promising,' he said approvingly, nodding at the glass bottle as he helped himself to a bowl and spoon.

'It's an orange liqueur,' Arielle informed him.

'Do you make it yourself?' he asked, helping himself to a generous scoop of raspberries and another of ice cream.

When had he last ate this simply? He did not know. What he did know was that it was surprisingly enjoyable.

She shook her head. 'No, my neighbours do. They have the equipment and the skill. But the oranges are from here. I've soaked the raspberries in it too.'

She filled the glasses, pushing one across at him. He took a cautious mouthful and blinked.

'It's strong,' she said unnecessarily. 'I've no idea what proof, but it's got a kick.'

'Very definitely,' Lycos said dryly, lowering the glass again. He looked across at her. 'This dinner has been very good, Arielle. You know, I think I will definitely keep you on as my personal chef,' he said.

He was baiting her and she reacted as he knew she would. Her face tightened, lips compressed. Very tender lips...

'So...' he went on, still in baiting mode, '...how do you intend to entertain me tomorrow?'

'I don't intend to entertain you in any way, at any time,' she said bitterly. 'I don't care what you do, *M'sieu* Dimistrios, tomorrow or any other day. I'll start packing up my personal belongings and I must go and see my neighbours about their taking the poultry. Then I must contact the local *lycée*, to collect the piano I'm giving them.'

He looked across at her. Her expression was closed, but there was something in the bleakness of her eyes she could not hide. Something that might have been tears welling. Something that made him speak.

'There's no rush,' he heard himself saying. 'Not for me. Nor you.'

He lifted up his liqueur glass, tilted it slightly at her and said, 'Why don't we just see how things turn out?'

Even as he spoke, he wondered at that too. Never, in his life, since he'd taken control of it as a teenager, had he ever held to such a pointless mantra. It ran counter to everything he lived his life by. Even when it came to the random turn of a card he did not hold by it. For in that card, whatever it was, he would make his calculation. His decisions based on that calculation. They were cold, careful decisions. Ruthless ones if necessary. But never made on impulse.

Except that it had been impulse that had made him turn off the highway and head off into this remote, deep countryside. Made him seek out the *mas* whose existence, let alone ownership, he had not known of this time yesterday.

And was it impulse now, saying what he just had?

See how things turn out...

The unfamiliar, alien words hung in his head. More thoughts formed. Questions.

What is it about this place that made me say that?

And it was not just this strangely peaceful *mas*. His eyes rested on the woman opposite him. Her face so beautiful. Her expression so sad.

He did not want her to be sad.

A frown flickered in his eyes. Why should he care if she was sad? Why should he care anything about her at all?

Or the home she was losing.

The place that was now his...

He drew his gaze away from her as she took some raspberries and began to eat them silently, still with that haunting sadness in her face. He eyes gazed out into the dark. The quietness of the garden and the surrounding countryside all about him. The scent of jasmine, the murmur of the cicadas, beguiling his senses. Inviting him to stay.

Slowly he lifted his liqueur glass to his lips and tasted,

again, the sweet, fiery distillate easing down his throat. His gaze returned to Arielle.

Lingering.

Questioning.

Beguiling his senses.

CHAPTER FIVE

ARIELLE WOKE. HER BEDROOM was full of sunshine. She hadn't drawn the curtains the night before, performing the minimum of bedtime ministrations, barely getting into her nightgown before sinking down on to her bed and drawing the bedclothes over her. Exhaustion had overcome her.

Emotional exhaustion from the cataclysmic events of the day and, too she knew, from the wine she'd drunk and that lethal liqueur.

As she came to consciousness now, she felt a fleeting longing that what had happened yesterday had only been a nightmare, unreal. But it was all too real. All too real a nightmare.

The *Mas Delfine* was gone, no longer her home. And she must leave and lose it for ever.

Words that the man who was taking it from her had framed themselves in her head.

You will survive.

Her face soured. Yes, of course she would survive. What choice did she have? None.

But survival would be bleak.

Heavily, she got out of bed. Judging by the sun, she'd

overslept by a good couple of hours and compunction smote her. The hens, and Maurice and Mathilde, would be desperate to get out. Hastily she pulled on the same clothes she'd worn yesterday and ventured out of her room, burningly conscious that at the other end of the landing was the man who was taking her beloved home from her. But she must not think of that right now. She must only hurry down to let out the poultry.

But as she unlocked the kitchen door and opened it, she stopped dead. The hens were already out. Jean-Paul, the very handsome, and very conceited cockerel who lorded over his harem, was strutting about, helping himself to the maize plentifully scattered over the cobbles. His harem was equally busily engaged.

'Have I given them too much?'

A voice from the gateway to the gardens made her head turn sharply. Lycos was strolling forward. For ten seconds Airelle could only stare. He was wearing a tee shirt, damp over his chest, and dark blue board shorts, his bare feet in open sandals. His sable hair was glistening wet.

'The pool was irresistible,' he said. 'And I wanted to beat Maurice and Mathilde to it.' He glanced at the poultry, greedily pecking away, the ducks joining in, as well as some opportunistic pigeons from the barn roof. 'I think I did overdo it,' he said ruefully.

Arielle laughed. She couldn't help it.

'You'll be their friend for life now,' she said dryly. 'Watch your toes!' she added sharply. 'Jean-Paul likes to remind everyone he's boss guy!'

Lycos stepped nimbly aside, as the cockerel headed purposefully towards him, wings stretching out.

'He knows you're male,' Arielle said.

'Please inform him…' Lycos said gravely, dark eyes glinting, '…that the only designs I might have on his harem is a culinary one.'

She gave another laugh, heading for the hen house. 'While they're feasting, I'll get the eggs gathered,' she said.

It seemed strange to be having any kind of civil conversation with Lycos Dimistrios, she thought as she started to check for eggs.

Maybe, though, it makes a hideous situation easier to cope with? Gives me a semblance of normality. However impossible…

Perhaps in anticipation of their very generous breakfast, the hens had laid well and she emerged some minutes later with a full colander. Lycos had disappeared, but when she went into the kitchen, she could hear the shower running. She set the colander of fresh eggs on the work surface and stared out of the window. Her mood was strange, how could it not be? Her thoughts were stranger. Outside the poultry were still making the most of the unexpected largesse. She took a breath. This time yesterday her world had ended. Lycos had walked into her life and smashed it to pieces.

Now…

It's still smashed. He might have let out the hens and fed them, and made himself at home in the pool—made himself at home, full stop—but he's invaded my life and taken it from me.

She felt her chest and throat tighten. But what could she do about it? Nothing. Nothing at all.

I have to cope with this. I knew it was coming. Gerald and Naomi made it clear. Relished making it clear. My days here are numbered.

And now the countdown had begun. Entirely at Lycos Dimistrios's timetable.

All I can do is bear it as well as I can.

Mechanically she got the coffee going, fetched milk from the fridge and set it to heat. From the ancient chest freezer, housed in what had been the old dairy but was now the utility with its old-fashioned washing machine, she removed a frozen baguette and some frozen croissants and popped them into the oven to thaw and warm through. Readying the breakfast tray made her chest tighten again. Putting out crockery and cutlery for two. Juicing some more oranges for them both. She might as well enjoy her oranges while she still had them.

'How did the egg collection go?' a voice behind her broke her painful reverie.

'Plenty for an omelette if you want one,' she said.

'Sounds good,' said Lycos. He leant against the door jamb. 'Any orange juice?'

Wordlessly Arielle poured a glass for him, then busied herself breaking eggs for omelettes and making coffee. Checking the milk heating in its pan on the stove, she got out a skillet and set the butter to melt for the eggs. The routine, mechanical movements kept her mind from thinking. Kept herself from thinking.

She removed the warmed bread and croissants from the oven, wrapped them in a clean tea towel and placed them on the tray, together with the freshly made coffee and hot milk in jugs. She handed the laden tray to Lycos, who had drained his orange juice.

'Take it out to the terrace,' she instructed. 'I'll be out with the omelettes in a minute or two.'

For a moment he did not move, as if she'd asked him something outrageous.

'I'm not your servant,' she said. 'If anything, I'm your guest,' she added sweetly, holding the tray towards him.

Wordlessly he put his empty glass on the worktop, took the tray and disappeared with it. She went back to the smoking skillet and poured in the beaten eggs, deftly spreading and lifting them as they cooked. Minutes later she was emerging on to the terrace with two plates, each with a folded omelette on them, which she deposited on the table.

'*Bon appétit*,' she said and got stuck in.

Lycos Dimitrios did likewise.

Together, under the bright morning sun, they ate. As they did, for reasons that made no sense at all, Arielle felt the tightness in her chest slacken. Imperceptibly, incomprehensibly, but slacken all the same.

Whatever it took to get her to bear what was happening, she would do it. Even if it meant being civil to the man who was taking her home from her.

'OK, where do I start?'

Lycos stood at the edge of the kitchen garden, surveying the scene beyond.

'Strawberries first, then raspberries, then peas, then beans,' Arielle said in response.

'Are we eating all that?' he asked.

'Either we do, or the birds will,' Arielle answered, heading towards the strawberry patch with her empty colander. She crouched down and made a start on lifting the leaves to check on the ripeness of the fruit beneath. She glanced back at him. 'If you don't pick any, you don't get to eat any. You're not eating mine!'

Resignedly, Lycos started on another row, hunkering down. Even dressed only in shorts and a tee shirt, he could feel that the morning was already hotting up. He glanced towards Arielle. She had put on a decrepit straw hat and, though it was fraying at the edges, it did the job of shading her head and neck. He kept his eyes on her a moment as she worked her way along her row. She couldn't see him looking at her and he was glad of it. It was extraordinary, he thought, that even dressed as she was, making no effort whatsoever to look good, she nevertheless looked extremely good.

Beautiful.

A kind of natural beauty. Unforced, effortless, unadorned. Her hair was caught back in a thick knot on the nape of her neck. Her slender forearms were honey-toned and her bare legs likewise. Her tee shirt was rounding her breasts in a very pleasing manner indeed.

He looked away. Thoughts were running through his head and blood was running through his veins. Coursing to places that were inappropriate for a morning dedicated to fruit and vegetable picking. He set them aside firmly and focussed on gathering the luscious looking ripe strawberries. After a while, his colander was full and he straightened up, stretching his back.

'Strawberries are the worst,' Arielle said, straightening up likewise. 'Raspberries are much easier. No stooping.'

So it proved and, although it took longer to fill his fresh colander on account of his sampling rather too many of the fruits he was picking, Lycos found it pleasantly relaxing. But then everything was proving pleasantly relaxing.

There was something about being in the fresh air with the heat of the sun beating down baking the earth and ripening its fruits. With no noise other than the ever-present chorus of cicadas beyond the kitchen gardens and the birdsong from songbirds chirruping from the sun-warmed walls against which pleached peach trees were espaliered. Something that really was very pleasant.

Very peaceful.

Very remote.

The world he knew seemed a long, long way away.

And he was glad of it.

Glad too, he realised, that he was not here alone, for there was something very companionable about working like this with Arielle nearby.

She seemed to have changed her attitude towards him. Was she accepting the inevitable now, that the *mas* was lost to her? The bristling hostility, the baleful expression in her eyes, had dissipated. Not completely, but he found he was glad of it all the same. Now she was being matter of fact, directing him to the next task.

'OK,' she announced. 'Time to tackle the peas and beans.'

She moved towards the serried rows of legumes, pausing only to toss down a handful of her picked raspberries onto the path, where almost immediately it was targeted by several of the waiting birds, who demolished the fruit in short order then retreated to the walls again to await more largesse.

Peas and beans were picked, Lycos attending to the former and Arielle the latter. They gathered up all their collective harvest, together with a head of lettuce, some tomatoes and a fistful of rocket. As they headed out, Arielle set down some strawberries for the birds. She closed the wooden gate securely as they left the kitchen gardens.

'Or the hens will wreak havoc!' she said. She headed back to the kitchen with Lycos following her.

'I've never picked my own lunch before,' he observed musingly.

'It makes it taste even sweeter,' she assured him.

He heard her words echo again as they settled down to lunch. Did it taste all the sweeter for his having picked and prepared so much of it himself? He fancied it did and the thought was pleasing to him. As pleasing as sitting here, in the fresh sweet air. Shaded from the heat of the sun by the faded awning, while he sank his teeth into the luscious ripe tomatoes, sprinkled with olive oil and salt, and helped himself to another slice of ham to go with the healthy portion of warm, lightly toasted bread, lavishly spread with creamy butter.

As pleasing, too, as letting his gaze settle, through half-lowered lids, on the woman sitting opposite him. His eyes rested on her. How effortlessly lovely she looked, even in clothes that were not designed to enhance her beauty. But there was an allure about her, natural and without design, that was drawing him. That had no art to it, no intent, no coquetry.

He felt the blood course through his veins yet again, admitting to himself that it was her difference to all the women he frequented, was familiar with, that was drawing him... Kindling in him a nascent desire that he saw no reason to deny, or diminish. Why should he?

She is here, and so am I. So why should we not indulge?

Why not indeed? He could think of no reason. He had time on his hands. Time that could be spent very pleasurably, exploring and experiencing, all that this so-totally-different woman had to offer him. Charming this beautiful, bucolic Cinderella...

His gaze shifted, going out over the peaceful, scent-filled gardens, to the lavender fields beyond, framed by the citrus and mulberry trees. Then it came back to Arielle.

She is part of this place. She goes with it.

And after all, he mused, since he had come here to take possession of this remote and unexpectedly his *mas*, why should he not take possession, too, of Arielle?

So very, very lovely...

He let his gaze continue to rest on her, taking pleasure in it. Confirmed in his resolve.

CHAPTER SIX

THE POWERFUL NOTE of the engine dropped to a smooth purr as Lycos steadied his speed along the highway. Arielle felt herself sink back into the deep, low-set passenger seat.

They were making for the old, walled, medieval town of Saint-Clément, popular with tourists in this part of Provence. Lycos said he wanted to get a feel for the area. He'd given her a cynical smile.

'Show me the sights, Arielle. It will mean you don't have to pack your bags and leave just yet,' he'd told her.

She had no more idea of why he wanted to play tourist than she had about why, for the past week, he'd continued to stay at the *mas*, making himself at home. She couldn't stop him, the *mas* was his. And even if she had to share the days with him, it meant she could have that much more time there too. And that was precious to her.

Yet it was so weird to have him there, day after day, apparently content to simply go along with her uneventful daily routine. His presence was getting easier to bear. Maybe she was just getting used to it. Getting used to having to accept that the *mas* was now his. That soon, all too soon, she would have to leave her home. Getting used to the anguish she felt over it.

Getting used to treating him civilly, without baleful hostility. As if he weren't the man taking her home from her.

But there was something happening to her that was distracting her from that. She felt it again, now, as her eyes slipped from watching the road ahead, to covertly glancing at Lycos's profile as he drove. She felt a little frisson go through her. It was becoming increasingly familiar and increasingly impossible to suppress.

She should suppress it, she knew. What did it matter that Lycos's dark looks could make her pulse quicken, her breath catch? And why should she care that sometimes she saw him watching her with something in his eyes that made the colour flush in her cheeks?

Yet something was happening. She knew she could not deny it, or suppress it. It was something that had nothing to do with the malign reason for his presence in her life.

She felt a little ache inside her. It had been so long since there had been anything like that for her. Her only big romance had been at music college, a fellow music student, a cellist, Ben, who had been taken on after graduating by a prestigious youth orchestra. She had not been so fortunate and that had been the year her mother's fatal illness had first made itself felt. So, they had gone their separate ways and she had come back to the *mas* to stay with her mother. To look after her, organise her treatment, then nurse her through her final months. It had not been a time for socialising, let alone romance. Then had come the turmoil of her father's remarriage, his early death, his disastrous will and her futile contesting of it…

To retreat, defeated. To make the most, the very most, of her last chance to live at the *mas*. The home she was to lose, however isolated she was there. Where none but her nearest neighbours ever occasionally came. No one else.

Until Lycos Dimistrios.

The frisson went through her again and she dragged her gaze away. Her thoughts disturbed. Disturbing…

Surely of all men it should not be the one taking her home from her that could make her react in that way? Be so susceptible to? But then she would remind herself that, just as Lycos himself had said to her, it wasn't him taking her home from her. It had never been hers at all.

It isn't Lycos's fault he owns it now.

So just as she could argue that she did not need to feel bitter and hostile towards him, maybe she didn't have to deny or suppress the effect he was having on her? Why not just acknowledge it, accept it?

The question hovered in her head. The temptation…

Her eyes slipped back to his profile again, where they wanted to go. A sense of release went through her, as if she'd finally given herself permission to do what she wanted to do. To let her gaze rest on the sinewed strength of his bare, tanned forearms, the curve of his fingers around the steering wheel effortlessly guiding the powerful car with the lightest of touches, his face in profile, eyes shaded by sunglasses. She felt that frisson come again, and this time made no attempt to resist it…

Facing the truth about herself. That there was something about Lycos Dimitrios that was more than just the man taking possession of her beloved home.

He was taking possession of her senses.

Lycos eased the car into a convenient parking space in a side road off the main square in Saint-Clément and cut the engine.

'Well, here we are,' he said conversationally. 'What is there to see first?'

'Probably the castle,' Arielle said.

They set off in that direction, Arielle leading the way. Half a step ahead of him, Lycos could rest his eyes on her at his leisure.

And his pleasure.

Because it really was very pleasurable to watch Arielle strolling lightly along. She'd abandoned her usual shorts and voluminous tee shirts and donned instead a flower-sprigged blue cotton dress. There was nothing special about it, it was obviously cheaply bought.

But it's she who makes it special.

His eyes flickered over her, taking in her slenderness, her natural grace, her slim waist, from which the soft swirl of her skirt fell in gathers to calf length. It wasn't low cut, but the sweetheart neckline and cap sleeves added to its appeal.

Added to her *appeal*, he mused.

She'd refrained from knotting her hair, catching it instead into a tendrilled switch with a length of blue ribbon. She still wore no make-up at all and he felt a sudden impulse to want to see her dressed to the nines, gowned in couture and with full *maquillage* and *coiffeur*. *En grande tenue*.

Then he banished it.

She does not need it.

Certainly not here, or now.

He went back to simply enjoying the vision she now was, the pleasure it gave him to behold it. To be with her.

Because that was strange in itself. He was used to women being either self-absorbed in their own appearance, or constantly making up to him and wanting to please him.

But Arielle is nothing like that. She pays no attention to herself and certainly makes no effort to please me.

Her initial baleful hostility towards him had eased off in the days since his arrival at the *mas*, but her attitude towards him was casual more than anything. So was his towards her. Just as he'd said that first evening, they were going with the flow.

This last week he'd done just that and wondered at it, even while he'd gone along with it. Day after peaceful unfolding day. Fitting, without effort or even decision, into the way Arielle lived her life, feeling the peace and quiet of the *mas* enfolding him. A way of life he'd never experienced before. Never even known existed.

Just as today was a novel experience for him too. A leisurely drive through the Provençal countryside dozing in the summer heat, to reach this old walled town and mingle with the tourists, with no purpose other than to pass the day pleasantly. A tour of the castle, with Arielle regaling him with tales of the interminable wars of the Middle Ages, was followed by lunch at a little *creperie* she took him to when he invited her to choose somewhere. The *crepes*, both savoury and sweet, had been humble, but tasty. Despite, or because of, them being nothing like his usual gourmet fare. Then they'd wandered along the narrow streets, mingling with tourists as Lycos never did, emerging into the picturesque central square that was dominated by a grand church. They'd toured the church, Arielle pausing to step aside and light a candle—for her mother, she'd told him.

Lycos had found himself strangely touched.

And envious.

To have a mother worth lighting a candle for...

He set the emotion aside. It had no place in his life.

They left the church and Lycos went back to doing what he was enjoying most in this surprisingly enjoyable day—looking at Arielle. She had become noticeably more at ease with him as the day progressed and he was glad of it. Glad of something else as well.

She is aware of me. As a woman is aware of a man. A man who is also aware of her in that way.

He was not laying it on strong. That would be crass and Arielle was not like that. And besides, the circumstances—his unwelcome presence at her home and the reason for it—meant that his first focus must be on lowering her guard against him. And that was happening. There were fewer barbed comments and less sadness in her eyes. This day out was proving a distraction for her. And that was welcome to him.

I want it gone. All that pain and stress and anger and anguish over the mas. *I want her to see only me, as I am.*

Not as the man taking her home from her. I do not want her to feel that grief over it any longer.

Yet, as they made their easy-going way across the square and his gaze returned to her once again, he could also acknowledge, as the peace and the quiet, the restful beauty of the *mas* these past days had shown him, how much she would grieve at its loss.

Who would not feel it? To lose a place like that.

Thoughts rose in his mind, flickering like candles. He had assumed he would turn the *mas* over to the realtors the moment he arrived in Paris. But was there any rush to do so? Why not simple keep possession of it for a while and enjoy it?

Enjoy the woman—this beautiful, artless, beguiling woman—who came with it?

It would give her longer there. The place she loves so much.

And give me her.

It was a pleasing thought. For both reasons.

Arielle gazed at the display of beautifully arrayed *pâtisserie* in the glass-topped counter.

'What will you choose?' Lycos asked as he stood beside her.

'So hard to decide,' she murmured. 'But I think the *tarte des pommes.*'

'For me,' he mused, 'I can't resist a slice of the *Gâteau St Honoré.*'

He relayed their choices and ordered coffee too. His French was fluent, she had come to realise during the course of the day, but it was distinctly accented. As was his English, in a way that, she had to acknowledge, added to the frisson that she kept experiencing in his company. It had not abated during the day. Just the opposite in fact.

What's happening to me? Why am I being like this? Reacting like this?

The question was foolish. She knew perfectly well why. Had known since that moment she had first seen him as he'd got out of his monster car. Still in his tuxedo, raffish with his rough jaw, tie loose, gazing around him in the early morning light, surveying his latest possession. Come to take it from her.

Because whatever his malign purpose, his impact on her had been, and was still now, like nothing she had ever experienced in her life. Powerful, pulse-quickening, making her aware of his masculinity in a way that was both disturbing and something else entirely, for exactly the same reason. Ben, her long-ago fellow music student, had been blond and hazel-eyed, dreamy and sensitive. Nothing like the lean, lethal Lycos Dimistrios. With his sable hair, his night-dark eyes, the lithe, muscled body she had seen ploughing effortlessly through the azure pool water and wading out in a shower of diamonds. Drawing her rivetted gaze and making her catch her breath.

Her gaze returned to him again, now, as they sat themselves down at a little marble-topped table under a shading awning on the wide pavement, awaiting their coffee and cakes. The *pâtisserie* was an upmarket one, directly edging the gardens that bordered the town's old ramparts, affording a vista out over the valley below, which was drenched in late afternoon sunshine. She let her gaze rest on him, indulging in the opportunity, as he surveyed the view.

His eyes returned to her. In the shade of the awning, he'd removed his dark glasses and his eyes met hers full on, knowing she'd been looking at him. She felt herself colour and saw his mouth quirk.

'A female who blushes. Can it be?' he murmured. There was a teasing note in his voice. Something more than teasing.

She swallowed. 'It's...it's just the heat,' she said.

'Indeed, even in the shade,' he murmured again. His eyes held hers still, washing over her. Heat rose in her cheeks again.

To her relief, the server was coming out, setting down what they had ordered. Arielle stirred her *café au lait*, willing her colour to subside. Lycos started on his *gâteau* and she likewise with her *tarte*.

'So, have you enjoyed today?' Lycos glanced at her.

She looked across at him. 'I thought today was for your benefit,' she said.

'For us both,' he said. 'And I have indeed enjoyed it. I've never been a tourist before, seeing a place just for the pleasure of it.' His tone was musing again.

She looked confused. 'But you've come from the Côte d'Azur. People only go there for pleasure!'

'I wasn't there for pleasure. At least, not for the pleasure of the place. I spend time there, but I don't sightsee. So today has been a novelty. A very pleasant one.' He took another forkful of his *gâteau*. 'This is very good,' he said. 'How about if I buy a whole one for us? For dessert tonight. Since we haven't picked any strawberries, or raspberries either.'

'If you like,' Arielle said. 'It's your call. I'm just the tour guide.'

His eyes held hers, an expression in them that threatened to make her flush again.

'You're more than that, Arielle.'

His voice was soft and his accent seemed more pronounced. Husky.

She looked away, breathless suddenly. She heard him give a low laugh—a laugh that made her all the more breathless, that threatened to flush the colour back into her cheeks and the heat into her veins. Then he called the server over as she finished serving another customer nearby. Arielle heard him request an entire *Gâteau St Honoré* to take away with them. It gave her time to gather her composure again. As much of it as she could. In her head she heard his words.

'You're more than that, Arielle.'

The frisson that she had felt throughout the day came again and she knew why.

Her eyes returned to him, feeling again that sense of breathless bemusement and that flush of betraying heat. Whatever it was about him, this man who had come out of nowhere to take her home from her, she was drawn to him for reasons she could not deny.

Nor do I want to.

The truth held in her head. Impossible to dismiss.

Whatever was happening, whatever was going to happen, that truth held. She did not know why this man, who spelt only disaster to her, could affect her as he did. Only that he did.

Thoughts flickered through her mind. Difficult ones. Ones she must face.

Perhaps it's helping me, this reaction to him. Perhaps it's allowing me, enabling me, to start what I know I must do. What he himself has told me I have to do. To accept that the life I have known till now is ending. Perhaps he can help me accept that.

Perhaps, the thought came now and with it a kind of sweet, poignant sadness, *he can be my swan song...*

Let her say goodbye to her home with something other than bitterness and anguish.

Something sweeter than that.

Lycos glanced at his watch. It was a favourite possession, bought in the first flush of his wealth. One of the many signifiers of that wealth that he had purchased since he had transformed himself into what he was. Right now, though, it was telling him something that had nothing to do with his wealth.

'We should probably make a move,' he said. 'The hens will be getting hungry for their supper. Speaking of which...' he looked across at Arielle, '...what do you say to a picnic-style supper for ourselves? Save on cooking. Do you know a good delicatessen hereabouts?'

She did, it seemed, and they made their way there, his purchases lavish. Then, leaving Arielle to go into a nearby *boulangerie*, he spotted a shop opposite that interested him. He emerged before Arielle did and waited for her on the pavement. They headed to where he'd parked his car, then drove along the narrow streets to leave the town. As he returned to the open road, changed gear and sped up, he relaxed back. He was glad to be heading back to the *mas*. He glanced across at Arielle beside him. Her hands were folded in her lap and she was looking out of the windscreen.

She looked effortlessly lovely.

He drove on, musing as to what his feeling was. It was strange to him. Then he identified it.

It was contentment.

A novel feeling. Strange to him indeed. A welcome one. A pleasant one.

And one that came with another. His glance went to Arielle again.

Anticipation.

He felt the feeling merge and mingle, uniting in him. Different from anything he'd known before.

But it felt good.

Better than anything he'd known before.

'Shut your eyes a moment. *Et voilà!*'

Arielle did as she was bid, then opened her eyes again. They widened even more as she saw what Lycos was holding out.

'Oh, how beautiful!' she exclaimed.

'Isn't it?' he agreed smiling. 'I saw it in the little shop across from the *boulangerie* and couldn't resist it. Here, let me try it on you.'

He stepped forward, the beautiful gossamer shawl, in myriad hues of blue and threaded with silver, was swirled around her shoulders. He stepped away again.

'Perfect,' he announced with satisfaction. 'I knew it would be. It matches your eyes. Do you like it?'

'Who could not?' Arielle replied. 'But I can't possibly keep it.' She started to undrape it, but he stopped her.

'Of course you can,' he said. 'It's a present.'

She looked at him. 'Why?'

'I am your guest,' he said. 'A guest should always give their hostess a present.'

Her lips pressed together. 'I'm not your hostess and you are not my guest. If anything, I am yours.'

'Don't be argumentative. And don't take off the shawl. The evening is a little chilly. Besides, I like to see you in it.'

His eyes rested on her and Arielle found she could not meet them. Found, too, that her pulse had quickened. There was no reason, none, for Lycos to give her anything at all. Let alone what was clearly a pricey gift, for she knew that little shop he'd got it from and it only stocked expensive items.

'Now...' he was continuing, drawing back her chair at the table as the dusk gathered, '...we shall toast our highly enjoyable outing today and plan what to do tomorrow.'

'Surely it's time for you to resume your journey to Paris?' Arielle said, taking her place, as he did likewise opposite her. The soft folds of the beautiful shawl nestled against her shoulders and upper arms. She knew it flattered her. For reasons she wasn't about to examine she'd made more of an effort this evening. She still wore the sun dress she'd worn during the day, but had added a simple necklace of blue beads and scooped her hair into an up style. Nothing formal, but graceful for all that.

Her lips had felt a little dry, so she'd glossed them with a slightly tinted gel and spritzed a light floral scent over her throat. She hadn't let herself think about the reasons, she'd just done it.

Her eyes went to him now, hearing her own question to him. Feeling, suddenly, a little dart of fear go through her.

I should want him to clear off to Paris and leave me here on my own for just a little bit longer.

But I don't.

Her expression changed. No, she did not want Lycos Dimitrios to go. To leave her.

So when he gave his answer, as he poured their wine handing one glass to her, she knew from her reaction that he had given the answer she should not want to hear and yet did want to hear at the same time.

'There's no rush,' he said easily. 'Paris can wait. This is far more pleasant.' He lifted his glass to her. '*Santé!* To a very enjoyable day. Thank you for being my tour guide.'

She gave a flickering smile, conscious of conflicting thoughts. Confusing thoughts. She dropped her eyes to the plates on the table, laded with the purchases from the delicatessen. *Charcuterie* and olives, a jar of caviar with blinis, poached chicken breasts and smoked trout, artichoke hearts and tiny stuffed peppers, *remoulade* and finely sliced tomatoes in a piquant vinaigrette, and assorted cheeses, together with the bread she'd bought.

Her gaze returned to him across the table, as she picked up her own glass. The dusky early evening, the soft glow from the table lamp, the light thrown from the parlour behind where they were sitting out on the terrace, all threw his features into *chiaroscuro*, highlighting them for her. She wanted to gaze and gaze, drink him in, but that would be far too obvious. So, she dropped her eyes instead, taking a delicate mouthful of her wine and setting back her glass on the table.

'What do we start with?' she asked, indicating the spread before them.

'Caviar,' Lycos pronounced, helping them both to generous portions. 'Do you like caviar?' he asked, making a start on his.

'It's not part of my everyday diet,' Arielle said wryly. 'I assume it is for you, though?'

He glanced across at her. 'Not always. I remember my first taste vividly. It was in my early days of making wins and I was flushed with success. I cashed in my chips and went to the bar to celebrate. Someone further down was having caviar and champagne, so I ordered the same.'

Arielle heard something change in his voice as he continued.

'I was on my way to a new life and I wanted to mark the occasion. That first taste of caviar put my old life behind me.'

There was an edge in his voice, she could hear that too. Then, abruptly, it was gone again. 'This should be such a moment for you too, Arielle. Putting your old life behind you. Walk away from the *mas*, head held high. Don't look back. I didn't. Nor should you.'

She felt her finger tighten around the knife she was using to lift caviar on to her blini.

'You don't understand—' she started. Her voice was as tight as her grip on the knife.

He cut across her. 'Arielle, move on! I did. I had to or I'd have gone the same way as my father—'

He broke off, swallowed his caviar and blini, reached for his wine, set the glass down with a click. Looked across the table at her.

'My father was not a stupid man,' he said. 'But he was weak and self-indulgent and self-pitying. He felt hard done by, so he drowned his sorrows. When his sense of frustration mounted, he took it out on me.'

She stared across at him. 'He...he hit you?'

'Until I got big enough to hit back. Then he stopped.'

'But...but what about your mother?'

'My mother?' Lycos's voice was harsh now. 'She'd walked out, fed up with his self-pity.'

'She left you with a father who hit you?' Arielle's voice was hollow.

'She went off with a man who didn't want any baggage.'

'But that's awful! How could she?'

'Very easily, apparently. But she'd never been much of a mother anyway. My memories are of her complaining vociferously to my father all the time. They only married because I was on the way. She left just after the economic crash in Greece came. My father lost his job—not that it was much of a job, but it brought in a wage at least—and then there were no more jobs to be had. But there was liquor to be had, so he took to that instead. Stayed with it to the end. He was a full-blown alcoholic by then. I took what care I could of him. Not that he noticed.'

He took a breath, looked right at her. 'Arielle, that's what I meant when I talked about responsibility and the freedom you have when you accept that you can't be responsible. I tried to stop my father drinking, felt responsible for him. But it wasn't my responsibility, it was his. And when I finally realised that, accepted it, I knew I was free. Free to walk away. So I did. He's dead now, long ago. As for my mother? I have no idea and don't care. Because she never cared about me either, so we're quits.'

He fell silent, helping himself to more caviar and another blini. Arielle looked across the table at him. Her emotions were mixed. It was hard to see Lycos Dimistrios—a man who'd turned up in evening dress and an uber-flash car, who clearly enjoyed a lavish lifestyle, who could win her family home on the casual turn of a card—as that bruised, bodily and emotionally, young boy. Abandoned by his mother. Growing into his teens to look after a violent, alcoholic father. Emotions plucked at her, but she did not know what they were, other than a natural pity for such an upbringing. The pain that must have caused him, even if he hid it now.

He looked across at her again. His face seemed closed now. Harder.

'So you see, Arielle, why I have limited sympathy for your plight. You may not have the inheritance you'd expected, but you're not penniless. You're young. You're healthy. You're beautiful. You're not going to have the life you thought you were going to have, but you can make a new one for yourself. That is, if you stop feeling sorry for yourself!'

'I'm *not*—' she started heatedly, ripped away from Lycos's sorry childhood to what consumed her.

'Yes, you are,' Lycos contradicted her. He took a

breath. 'Arielle, self-pity gets you nowhere. I should know. But neither does anger and resentment. I know that too. Looking back doesn't help, only looking forward. Like I've already said to you, if this place means that much to you go off and do what I did. Make a fortune somehow, anyhow, and buy it back. It will be for sale for the right price. Everything...' his voice turned cynical '...is for sale at the right price.'

He reached for his wine, took a deliberate mouthful and set back the glass. He looked across the table at her again.

'OK, subject closed. Let's move on and enjoy the present. So, do you like caviar?' He raised a quizzical eyebrow.

Under his scrutiny she took a mouthful of caviar and blini. Testing it out.

She nodded. 'Yes,' she said.

He smiled. It relaxed all his features. Made him less forbidding, less censorious.

'Eat up then or I'll polish it all off! Now, as I was saying, how shall we spend tomorrow? After a day out, my vote is for a lazy day here. Join Maurice and Mathilde in their pool,' he said good-humouredly.

He reached for more caviar, glancing across at Arielle again as he did. He gave a nod of approval.

'Yes, I chose well,' he said satisfied. 'That shawl becomes you perfectly! How beautiful you are, Arielle. So incredibly beautiful.'

He had not changed his voice as he paid her the compliment, but Arielle could not stop the flush running out into her cheeks. He gave a low laugh. The laugh that told her things she should not want to hear, yet knew she did.

She dropped her head, confused and self-conscious. Her pulse had quickened and the colour in her cheeks was not subsiding. She reached for her wine, looking up as she did. His eyes were resting on her and in the uncertain light there was a glint in them that only made her pulse quicken even more.

The glint of a wolf—

Lycos saw her react to him. It was what he wanted. He wanted her to move on from her endless obsession with her lost inheritance.

Move on to me, to what I want of her. And to what she wants too, if she only admits it.

She was on the way, he knew. Calling her out, as he had just then, seemed to have worked. She had visibly relaxed again and they went on enjoying the delicacies procured in Saint-Clément. For a moment he frowned inwardly. What he had told her about himself he had never told a living soul.

So why tell her?

He brushed the question aside, letting his eyes rest on her instead, feeling a reaction go through him that was becoming increasingly familiar. Increasingly welcome. She really was so very lovely, so very beautiful, so very appealing to him.

He got to his feet, starting to clear the table. Arielle made a move to help, but he stopped her.

'No. Let me,' he said.

She acquiesced and he made short work of carrying

out the used plates and leftovers to the kitchen, putting the former in the sink and the latter in the fridge. Minutes later he came back outdoors. The night had gathered in earnest now and Arielle was sitting with her back to him, her hair limned with gold from the light of the wall lamp and the glass-sheltered candle on the table. She was relaxed back in her chair, the colourful shawl he'd bought for her gathered around her shoulders, exposing the delicate nape of her neck. He could not resist. He paused behind her and, before she could turn her head, he'd dropped the lightest of kisses on her nape.

He felt her still, heard her breath catch.

He straightened again.

'I come bearing sweet delight,' he informed her as he placed on the table a large, square cardboard box, secured with ribbons and bearing the ornate name of the *pâtisserie* where they'd had coffee. He opened it with a flourish.

'*Gâteau St Honoré!*' he announced portentously. Then he frowned. 'I have no idea how to slice it without making a complete hash of it!'

Somehow, he managed it, to Arielle's smiling applause, giving them both generous, if slightly messy, portions. He watched as Arielle lifted a full forkful of the *gâteau* to her lips and took a mouthful. A low moan of bliss came from her and her eyelids fluttered shut as she relished the experience, her expression transfigured.

Out of nowhere, a dart of arousal possessed Lycos.

She will look like that when her moment comes in my arms...

'Oh, that is so *good*!' sighed Arielle, taking another forkful. 'This was an inspired purchase! Thank you!'

'You are most welcome.' Lycos smiled, getting stuck into his own luscious portion, indulging a more immediate appetite.

Slices demolished, they both went for seconds, and it was a sadly depleted *gâteau* that remained by the end of the meal. Arielle sat back with an air of repletion about her.

'I'll go and make some coffee,' she announced.

'I'll give you a hand,' Lycos offered companionably. 'And why don't we move to the comfy chairs?' he nodded at the two padded cane armchairs with footstools just by the French window to the parlour. 'If we turn off all the lights, we can look at the stars.'

That was exactly what they did and Lycos found it pleasingly relaxing. In the soft night there was no sound beyond the incessant cicadas, the occasional call of a night bird and the distant faint sound of a church clock striking from the village several kilometres away. He'd moved the two chairs next to each other. Once Arielle had placed her empty coffee cup on the stone paving, she'd rested her hands on the chair arms and relaxed back against the head rest.

Lycos did likewise. Except that his hand, adjacent to Arielle's, did not rest on his own chair arm. He let it fold, lightly and casually, over Arielle's. For a second he felt her tense, then it was gone. He did not move his hand. Her hand was warm beneath his covering palm. Deliberately he did not look at her. Instead, he lifted up his other hand to gesture towards the night sky, ablaze with stars.

'Another van Gogh night,' he said.

He let his hand go on resting over hers. Let her get used to the sensation of his innocuous touch.

'Poor Vincent,' she replied. 'He had such a sad life, but I think he was happy here in Provence.'

'It's an easy place to be happy,' Lycos said.

'Yes,' she said softly. 'It is.'

And then, quite distinctly, Lycos felt her hand turn beneath his, and her fingers mesh with his, easing into holding his hand. Slowly, very slowly, he let his thumb softly stroke hers. Not making a big thing of it, just letting it happen...

Peace filled him. It was good, so very good, just to lounge here holding Arielle's soft hand, relaxed and replete, quietly and easily. Gazing up at the starry, starry night. Listening to the cicadas, wrapped in the warmth of the summer's soft darkness.

CHAPTER SEVEN

WHY HAD SHE taken Lycos's hand like that? The question hung for a moment in Arielle's thoughts, then she let it go. What did reasons matter? She had done it without thinking. It seemed right to do. Natural.

His hand was warm. Warm and strong. Meshing with hers. Uniting them.

Which was strange, illogical, as there was nothing to unite her and Lycos. He was taking her home away from her. She should remember that.

But right now, somehow, beneath those golden stars glowing through the dark floor of heaven, that did not seem to matter. It seemed extremely far away. A strange, dream-like state was enveloping her, filled with the heady perfume of the jasmine, the velvet warmth of the night, the wine in her veins. With her free hand she fingered the soft folds of the lovely shawl, soft around her shoulders, his gift to her. In her head she heard his words to her, telling her she was beautiful.

She felt, at the nape of her neck, the soft brush of his mouth as he'd kissed her so lightly, so briefly. Felt too, now, the warmth of Lycos's hand holding hers, felt her head turn towards him.

He was looking at her. His eyes, dark, unreadable, seen only by starlight, boring into hers. She could not look away. It was impossible to do so. Emotion welled up in her. Emotion she did not know, did not recognise. Emotion she could not, would not, name. She only knew that it was filling her, taking her over. Making that shimmering memory of his light, brief kiss on the nape of her neck a million times more shimmering. She felt her heart jump, her breath catch. Felt her fingers tighten in his—his tighten in hers. He leant towards her. His dark eyes boring into hers. There was a drumming in her ears, a quickening in her veins. She was breathless and motionless, just gazing into his eyes. She caught the scent of his aftershave, the scent and warmth of his body. She felt the warmth of his breath and then…

She heard her name, breathed like a wisp of air, then heard no more. Only felt, as her eyes fluttered shut, the soft, slow, languorous velvet of his mouth on hers, reaching for her. So soft, so slow. Tasting her lips, brushing them like silk.

She felt her free hand lift to where it wanted, no needed, to go. Her fingers curved around the nape of his neck and splayed out into his dark hair.

She held his mouth to hers as hers opened to his. It was impossible not to do so. Impossible to resist. Impossible not to give a low, soft moan as the wonder and the pleasure and the sweetness of it filled her so completely.

How long they kissed she did not know, for time had stopped, the world had ceased and everything had been lost in the sweet, honied pleasure he was drawing from her. The pleasure that was quickening in her. It filled her being, filled her veins, pulsed through her.

His hand tightened on hers. He drew her to her feet and she did not resist at all. Why should she resist this? Why, when it was all she wanted and it was the most wonderful thing in all the world to be kissed by Lycos in the warm velvet night, beneath the star-filled arc of the heavens.

His mouth drew away and a cry of loss broke from her, but his eyes, so dark and so drowning, were still fixed on hers. A smile was on his lips, as his long lashes dipped over his eyes. Wonder filled her, consumed her, possessed her infinitely and consumingly.

'Come to me, Arielle,' his voice was soft, low and filled with something she could give no name to, but knew at the deepest level of her being. Knew, recognised and shared, for it was in her as well.

'Come to me because you are so, so beautiful. Because I am filled with desire for you. Because you are all that I want.' His invocation was in his words. His voice. 'Come to me.'

And Arielle came.

Willingly, joyfully, with wonderment. And with a soft, warm fire lighting within her. Kindling a soft, warm flame that set her whole body aglow. Aglow for this man who had come into her life without expectation, or preparation. Who had seemed to be only the man who would take her home from her. And yet, somehow now—through the sweep of his darkening gaze, the husk of his voice, the touch of his hand, the velvet of his mouth—he had become someone she welcomed with all the quickening of her pulse.

His mouth closed over hers again, drawing from her yet more sweetness, the honey of arousal. He relinquished her only to lead her—eyes holding hers, her hand fast in his—into the house, through the hallway, up the echoing stone stairs and along the wood-floored corridor to open the door to his bedroom.

In that moment, he was all that she desired.

All.

She breathed his name as he drew her inside his bedroom, took her into his arms again.

'Lycos.'

It was the breath of night, of stars, of sweet, sweet desire.

And she yielded to it with all her heart.

Her slender body was pliant in his embrace, the softness of her breasts swelling as his hand folded around the nape of her neck, holding her for his kiss. It was slow and sensuous, and arousing. For her and for himself. He felt himself harden against her. Heard, and felt, the tiny gasp from her throat as his desire for her became tangible. A low laugh broke from him, as husky as his voice.

'Do you want me to hide what you do to me?' he said against her lips, his free hand moving down her back to pull her more tightly against him. He could feel her soft breasts responding to the feel of the his chest, raising his own level of arousal—and hers. He wanted more.

His kiss deepened, opening her mouth with his, his tongue twining with hers. She leant into him, head going back, hips pushing against his, strengthening his own arousal. His hand left the nape of her neck and moved down to the neckline of her dress instead. He moved it down, exposing her bra, her hardened nipples visible. Deftly he peeled the unnecessary fabric away, and her beautiful, engorged breasts spilled out. Arousal rose again and his mouth dipped to make its feast.

Another gasp came from her throat as, with lips and tongue, he teased and laved. She moaned again, head dropping back, breasts bared, uplifted to his ministrations. It was good. So very good. But he wanted more.

His hand at her back reached up for the zip of her dress, drawing it down in one long, smooth glide. It fell to the floor, and she stepped out of it. He unfastened her peeled down bra and discarded it carelessly. Now she was naked to the waist. He stepped back a moment, both hands resting now on the curve of her hips, surveying her. How very, very lovely she was, with her engorged breasts, straining nipples, glorious hair cascading over her shoulders, lips parted. And in her eyes...

The flame of desire.

Slowly, very slowly, he ran a finger along the waistline of her panties. Her breathing was shallow, pupils dilated. He lowered his hand, palming the soft mound beneath. He felt her stance change...widening. He gave another low, husky laugh. Let his hand move lower still. She gave a gasp that became a moan.

For a moment he toyed with her, feeling his own arousal mounting yet higher. He wanted more.

With a sudden movement he pulled her panties down her legs, wanting her entirely naked. She kicked them away herself, standing there in front of him, bared to the starlight. And to him.

Slowly, methodically, never taking his eyes from her, he peeled off his polo shirt and dropped it to the floor. Then he unfastened his belt, shucked off his chinos and his boxer shorts, and stood in front of her, as naked as she.

Her eyes were fixed on him—then dipped to his waist. Below his waist. He gave his low laugh again and reached for her hand.

'You see what you do to me?' He moved her hand to himself.

He heard her say his name, a whisper. Lifting her hand away, he led her to his bed.

Lycos laid her down. Her heart was racing, her breathing shallow. Blood coursing. Desire pouring through her. The way he'd kissed her, touched her, brought her to touch him, was feeding a want in her that was impossible to extinguish. But why should she? This was what she wanted, what she was giving herself to. Yielding completely.

He lay down beside her, kissing her again, deeply and sensually. His hand cupped her straining breast, nipple between his fingers. Scissoring, pinching lightly, until she thought she must go mad with it. Then performing the same with her other breast. His body was moving over hers and she could feel her thighs slacken. Feel his strong, muscled thigh moving over hers. Feel more than his thigh...

His hand was leaving her breast, sliding down over her body, sliding between her thighs. She moaned again, as he found what he wanted to find. What she wanted him to find. She was getting closer, she could feel it. As his fingers glided between the soft, silken folds of her body, she moaned again. She heard him give his low laugh, knowing what he was doing to her, drawing from her. Restlessness was taking her over and yet, though each skilled stroke of his fingers was a deliciousness she could barely bear, it was not enough.

Her legs moved, trying to capture his, to draw him across her. His name broke from her again, hungry, urgent. She could feel the response of her body to his intimate touch building inexorably and she was unable to quench it. Nor did she want to. It felt too good. Too blissful. Too tormentingly arousing.

But she did not want...

Her hands went to his shoulders, pulling him down on her. Wanting the pressure of his strong, hard body on her. Widening her legs, lifting her hips, inviting him. Imploring him...

Her nails dug into his shoulders, neck lifting, muscles tightening. Hunger growing.

'Lycos, please. I can't...'

He looked down at her, a smile playing at his mouth, his eyes half-lidded. Her nails dug deeper, hips lifted higher. This was a torment, a hunger she needed to sate. A desperation.

His smile deepened. 'Is this, my beautiful Arielle, what you want?'

He slid his fingers from her, with the flat of his hand widening her thighs, moving over her completely.

'Allow me to oblige,' he said with a smile.

He entered her straining, yearning, imploring body in one strong, powerful thrust. With what remained of her conscious mind, which had turned to mush under his skilled and tormenting caresses, she meant to warn him that it had been a long, long time since she had last known intimacy with a man. That her body was out of practice.

But any warning was as unnecessary as it was unsaid.

He had prepared her well.

She gave a gasp as he thrust into her.

He filled her. Absolutely and completely, their bodies fusing into one. And as they fused, glory took her.

It swept over her. Swept up from the very heart of her, to possess her totally. A single glorious, incandescent flame that burst within her. She cried out. She was pulsing around him. Enveloping him, enclosing him, drawing him further and further into her. She could feel her body fusing around his, feeling his strength, his flesh becoming her own flesh. She cried out again. The burning glory of it, the wonder, the ecstasy. His name broke from her lips, over and over again. Her hands slid around his back and pressed into him, holding him as closely as she held him within her.

She could feel him shuddering within her. Heard him cry out too. She was rocking against him now to keep the glory, that endless ecstasy, pulsing and pounding through her.

She was not crying out now. Now sobs were breaking from her throat and her spine was bowing. Thighs wrapped around him, neck arching forward. Pressing him to her, never to let him go...

How long it lasted she did not know. Only that slowly, infinitely slowly, she was coming down. The ecstasy possessing her was becoming an echo. A sweet, sighing echo. She felt her straining muscles relax across all her body, her thighs loosening. Yet she did not relinquish him. She held him close still, close within her, though his muscles had slackened too. She felt him lift himself on one elbow, saw him looking down at her with a softness in his eyes. His hand smoothed the tangled locks of her hair away from her face. His mouth brushed hers.

'Arielle,' he said with a voice that was as soft as the light in his eyes. As soft as the touch of his hand. 'My beautiful, beautiful Arielle.'

She saw his long, dark lashes lower over his eyes, heard the sigh of repletion, of passion fulfilled, in his breath. Heard his breathing slow. His head lowered to her shoulder and, as her hand folded around the strong nape of his neck, her own breathing slowed. Her eyes fluttered shut and she joined him in sleep. Sweet, satiated and complete. Holding Lycos in her arms.

The only place she wanted him to be.

Lycos padded back to the bed from the bathroom. Dawn was approaching and already the night sky was paling. He could see Arielle outlined beneath the coverlet he'd pulled over them both at some stage of the night. She was still asleep. He was not surprised. Their night had been...

Active.

To possess her once had not been sufficient. Though could anything exceed that first incredible union? He had known his desire for her had been certain and strong. But she had shown him a hunger of her own for him that had been like a burning brand, igniting him with a flame that seared him in a single thrust of his body. The intensity of his response had been something he'd never experienced before.

Because she gave herself to me. Hungered for me.

Her desire for him came from herself—natural, ardent and passionate.

She is like no other woman.

He folded himself down beside her, drawing her sleeping body against his, hearing her murmur as he did. Her body was soft against his, moulding back against him. His arm held her close, her scent beguiling him. Drawn back against him, he felt her closeness start to have its inevitable effect on him. But he let it die away. He, too, needed more sleep yet.

Passion could flame again when the sun arose.

And it could fill their days and their nights. But for now, sleep was all he wanted.

And Arielle in his arms.

Lycos stretched languorously on the sun lounger by the pool. 'Mmm. That feels good,' he said. Arielle was massaging sun cream onto his back. The slow, warm, ultra-sensuous strokes of her palms were very good indeed. And all too easily arousing.

He changed his thoughts quickly. There was time enough for that later. A lot more time. Any amount of time in fact.

As much time as I want.

And, right now, what he wanted was this. Just this. Here at the *mas*. Long leisurely days, long sensual nights. No rush, no agenda, no demands, no diversions. Simply to enjoy what was happening.

*Being here. Slowing down. Taking things easy.
With Arielle.
Going with the flow.*

And the flow was good, very good. Simple, leisurely, detached from anything going on anywhere else. He felt himself relax into the slow, sensuous massage that Arielle was giving him as she perched beside him on the lounger. The feel of her hip indenting into his. The scent of her body—a body he now knew so, so intimately—caught his breath and mingled with the rich aroma of the sun cream she was smoothing into his sun-warmed skin.

The soft palm strokes ceased.

'Don't stop,' he murmured.

'You're all done,' said Arielle. He could hear the smile in her voice, as she stood up. 'Time for a cooling drink.'

Lycos watched her go. Her natural grace, the unconscious sway of her body, so alluring even without her realising it, all held his gaze. As she disappeared through the stone gateway, he let his gaze lift to the sky. The afternoon sun was still high, tiny cloudlets puffing to the west, warmth flooding through him. So peaceful. So quiet.

Even the ducks were quiet. Maurice and Mathilde were nestled down in the shade on the far side of the pool, their heads buried in their folded wings as the pool water gently lapped against the filter.

Only the ever-invisible cicadas seemed to be active, along with a few butterflies that were busying themselves with the lavender bushes against the old stone wall and a bird that was pecking randomly in a flower bed.

Peace and quiet. Quiet and peace. It soaked into the

warm stone of the house, the garden wall, the paving around the pool. Soaked into the lavender-scented air.

It soaked into him.

He let his eyes close, the brightness of the sun pressing on his lids. He wondered what he was thinking and then realised he wasn't thinking anything at all. Only that this was good. This moment. This day. This time.

Time that seemed to have almost stopped. Turning over slowly, unhurriedly, uncounted. Turning with the hours of the day, the setting of the sun, the rising of the moon and the pricking out, one by one, of the gold stars in the dark velvet night. Easing towards the morning and the sun lifting in the east, its rays stealing over the roofs of the barns, threading through the canopy of the sheltering trees, awakening the birds, rousing the hens and the ducks from their night's slumbers.

Rousing him and Arielle, from their entwined arms, their tangled legs, their desire-sated bodies. To start the day all over again.

How long he had been here at the *mas* he scarcely knew and did not care. He only cared that Arielle was here and time had ceased.

Arielle crossed to the sofa, snuggling down beside Lycos, piano abandoned. At his invitation she often played for him after they'd dined, notes rippling soothingly as he relaxed on the sofa, watching her through half-closed eyes. Now, the final nocturne finished, she joined him. He put his arm around her and pulled her close against him. His long legs stretched out, crossed at his ankles, free hand cupping his liqueur glass. She reached to take a tiny sip herself from it. How strange it felt sometimes to be so intimate with him, even in little gestures like that. How strange and yet how entirely natural.

As if it has always been like this.
And always will be.

A shadow flickered in her eyes as she rested her head against his shoulder. But it wouldn't always be like this, would it? She had given herself to Lycos. To her own consuming desire for him, that glowed within her like a sweet, sweet flame. And to his desire for her that made that flame burn so wondrously.

But for how long would that flame burn?

She did not want to think about it. Did not want to do anything other than accept what had happened, feel wonder that it had and feel this deep contentment that filled her every moment of every day. Every gold-limned day.

Here, with Lycos.
While he wants me.

While it pleased him to stay here, at the *mas*, with her. Day after timeless day.

She felt him drop a light kiss on her hair.

'Today was good,' he said.

She tilted her face to him. 'It was, wasn't it? And you truly didn't mind my dragging you along?'

He laughed—a relaxed, indulgent sound. 'My first grape harvest,' he mused.

'You did well,' she praised him. She'd responded to a call by her neighbours, Jeanne and Claude, saying they were shorthanded that day. She always lent a hand when they asked, exchanging her labour for wine. She'd passed the request on tentatively to Lycos, but he'd volunteered willingly. They'd driven over in the morning and pitched in all day.

They'd then shared the communal evening meal Jeanne had prepared for all the workers. Again, Lycos had joined in cheerfully. Arielle had been aware that Jeanne's knowing eyes had taken in that she and Lycos were on more than friendly terms. But she'd said nothing, and for that Arielle was grateful.

She had been glad, too, that Lycos had been civil and neighbourly to the couple whose land neighboured that of *Mas Delfine*. She hoped it meant he would not sell the *mas* to new owners who would not be good neighbours to Jeanne and Claude. She pushed the thought away. The time would come when the *mas* was no longer her home, but for these precious final days, however long they lasted, she would not let thoughts of the future spoil this golden time.

My swan song, made possible because of what has happened between Lycos and myself. Giving me good memories of this last time here, instead of sad ones.

For that she would be grateful to Lycos. As for anything more...

She must not ask. This must be enough.

He was speaking again and she paid attention.

'Would you mind if I abandon you tomorrow morning?' he asked. 'I've promised to take young Daniel out for a spin in my car.'

Arielle's face lit up. Daniel was Jeanne and Claude's son, home for the harvest. The lad had been instantly wowed, and dead impressed, when she and Lycos had arrived in Lycos's growling monster.

'Oh, that's so kind of you!' she exclaimed warmly. 'He'll be your fan for life!'

Lycos laughed. 'He's a nice kid,' he said.

She brushed his cheek with her lips. 'And you are a nice man, Lycos Dimistrios,' she said softly, warmly, her eyes aglow. 'A good man.'

He met her eyes, a curious light in his. 'Good?' he echoed. 'I've not been called that before,' he said slowly.

For an instant that strange look held in his eyes. Then it changed. Became very familiar.

And its effects were very familiar.

She felt her breath quicken, her pulse quicken, her lips part.

His kiss was sensuous, arousing. She heard him deposit his liqueur glass. Felt him shift position and get to his feet, scooping her up into his arms as he did so. She gave a cry that was half laugh, half gasp.

He kissed her again, more deeply, more arousing. Eyes devouring hers. Heavy-lidded and with one expression, one purpose, in them only.

'Bed,' he said. The single word was a husk and a growl, and a promise that made her insides melt.

CHAPTER EIGHT

Lycos was looking at his phone, a slight frown on his face. Out of nowhere a sliver of unease coursed through Arielle. She paused in the act of beating fresh eggs, gathered that very hour from her obliging hens, ready to make a breakfast omelette. A late breakfast, for passion had overcome them before rising—as it so often did.

He put his phone aside on the dresser, but his frown remained.

'What is it?' Arielle asked, eyes resting on him. A cold feeling of apprehension crept over her.

She knew what she feared. That this golden time, this sweet swan song to ease her parting from her home, was ending. Her time with Lycos was ending.

She felt a fear stab at her. Did it come from knowing she must leave her home for ever? Or from the thought of losing Lycos for ever?

Both must happen.

But must it be now, this very morning?

For a moment, the memory of standing out in the courtyard the day Lycos had arrived to take away all that she held dear burned in her head.

But now it is not just my home that I hold dear...

She felt her mind shy away, unwilling to confront that truth. Yet knowing it was there, all the same.

Because how could it not be? She could tell herself all she liked that this time with Lycos must only be transient, to ease her to the new life that must await her when he no longer wanted her and she no longer had the *mas* to call home.

But now, as he looked at her with his expression shuttered, she could feel the protest rise within her. Protest that this golden time with him was ending.

Not yet, oh, please, not yet!

The cry came from deep inside her. A place she dared not acknowledge but felt all the same. A dread, an anguish, a loss.

For a moment Lycos did not speak.

'I may need to go to Paris,' he said. His voice was clipped.

Arielle felt her face pale. It had come out of nowhere, Lycos walking out of her life. Just as he had walked into it from nowhere. Emotion clutched at her, but she would not name it. Dimly, as if from far away, she realised he was speaking still.

'I told you I was on my way there originally for a meeting with the banker who handles my finances. He's just texted me to say that he will need to fly to Germany shortly. Another client has need of him. That he will probably be there a while, then move on to Prague and Vienna. So, if I still want to see him, next week would be a good time.'

Arielle swallowed. It was painful, but she made herself say what had to be said.

'Then you must go,' she said.

He frowned again, brows drawing together. It gave him a forbidding look.

'I don't want to, but I think I must. I've delayed too long already. Except that—'

He broke off. His gaze went to the window, where the sun was filling the courtyard and the hens were wandering around pecking here and there. Then his gaze returned to her.

She waited for the words. The words she knew would come, must come. She had heard them already. Knew what they would be. He would be kind and tactful, but he would say them all the same.

'It's been good, Arielle, this time with you. Here at the mas, *here with you. But now it's time for me to leave, to go back to my own life. And you, for you it is time to leave too. To start your new life. I wish you well. We'll both have good memories of this time now. Good memories.'*

And memories were all that she would have. Nothing more. Memories of her home. Of Lycos.

Nothing more than memories.

'So, what do you say?'

She blinked. What had he just said?

'Arielle?' He lifted a hand, waved it as though to wake her. His expression was strange. She couldn't make it out.

He spoke again.

'How do you feel...' he said to her, his eyes resting on her with that strange expression in them, '...about coming to Paris with me?'

* * *

Lycos kept his gaze steady on her. Her expression was blank. 'Arielle?' he said again.

She stared at him blankly then said, 'You're asking me to come to Paris?'

She said it as if he'd spoken in a foreign language.

Lycos nodded. 'Yes. Would you like to?'

Uncertainty filled her face now. It made him feel unsure too. Surely she would want to come with him. Wouldn't she?

Abruptly, he felt doubt shape itself in his mind. Intruding. Unwelcome. He desired Arielle, of that he had no doubt at all. He had desired her from the first moment he'd seen her. Had focussed on fulfilling that desire. And now he was focussed on continuing to fulfil it. He wasn't in the least bored or tired of her. He wanted her now as much as he had wanted her from the first. He had no idea how long that desire would last, but while it did, he did not wish to part with her.

Surely she feels the same? She is as ardent as she was that very first night. As passionate. I see it in her eyes, her face, the ecstasy of her body.

So why this hesitation now?

Unless—

He felt a sliver of cold penetrate. A thought even more unwelcome than that dart of doubt pushing into his consciousness.

Did she give herself to me because it meant I would let her stay on at the mas, *here with me?*

Instantly he refuted it, yet the echo remained. The intrusive corollary.

Is it me she wants? Or her precious mas?

Again, he pushed the thought aside, thrust it from him. He would not allow himself to think it. Would not even allow himself to wonder why he asked it. Why it disturbed him so.

She was speaking again. That same look of uncertainty, confusion, still on her face.

'I'm not sure what you mean,' she said. 'I have to pack up my things here. Leave the *mas*. Go to England.'

He felt the disturbing question in his head set aside. Focussing now on driving forward towards the goal he sought—Arielle's acquiescence to what he wanted. Taking her to Paris and having her there with him.

This time at the mas *with her has been good, so very good. A relaxing escape. A pastoral idyll. But it cannot last for ever and I need to pick up my own life. My old life.*

Besides, he wanted to take Arielle to Paris. Wanted to show her the bright lights and the luxury life he led. The one he had made for him himself, won for himself. He wanted to bestow it on her.

He lifted one eyebrow. 'Why not stay with me in Paris first?'

He felt his thoughts start to run ahead. He'd wondered what Arielle's beauty might be if she actually paid attention to it. Well, in Paris he would find out. He'd take her to the couture houses, get her properly dressed and gowned. Get her hair done, her face done. Get everything done. Buy her some jewellery.

Then take her out and about with me.

A sense of anticipation arose in him. But she was still looking uncertain. He wanted to push past that.

'We'll sort things out here before we set off. Tell Jeanne and Claude they can collect the poultry whenever they want. I'll arrange for your piano to go to the *lycée* before I sell. As for your things, just pack what you need for Paris and for England. Everything else can stay boxed up in the barns and I'll have it all sent to England when you're settled there.'

She still looked confused, dazed even. He walked over to her. Took the egg whisk out of her hand. Took her hands in his and turned her towards him. He looked down into her eyes, his gaze full.

'I want you with me in Paris, Arielle,' he said. 'I've lived your life here with you at the *mas*. Now come to Paris with me and live my life! You'll enjoy it, I promise.'

Her expression became troubled.

'I can't afford your life, Lycos,' she said.

He shook his head impatiently. 'You don't have to. It's all on me, Arielle. Of course it is! You'll be my... my guest, if you want to put it that way! You've already told me you're my guest here at the *mas*, since I own it, so what's the difference about being my guest in Paris?'

His mouth pulled at the corner with the slightest twist and a glint in his eyes. 'I'm a rich man, Arielle. I can afford to treat you. Treat you to anything you want. To anything I want to give you!'

His expression lightened. 'I want to show you Paris, Arielle.' His hands pressed hers. 'And I want to show you to Paris! I can't wait to do so.'

There was a huskiness in his voice, a tone of anticipation. He could see her expression wavering. He bent his head and kissed her softly. Slowly and seductively. He lifted his mouth from hers.

'Say yes, Arielle,' he said to her. His eyes were warm, his voice warmer.

Softly, he brushed her lips once more. Teasingly, temptingly. Willing her to yield to what he wanted of her.

'Say yes,' he said again.

Arielle leant against the windowsill and sighed with pleasure. Their room in the smart, boutique hotel overlooked the River Seine, flowing around the exclusive Île Saint-Louis in Paris. If she looked north, she could see the dramatic bulk of Notre-Dame and across the river she could see the fabled Left Bank. In the light of the setting sun, the river's water was turning to liquid gold. A couple of *bateaux mouches* glided peacefully along.

'Like it?' asked Lycos, his voice warm.

She turned. 'Oh, yes!' She sighed with pleasure.

'I'm glad. I've stayed here before and I like the Île Saint-Louis. It's exclusive, but quiet. Out of the way, yet central enough for me.'

He leant beside her on the windowsill, the window thrown open. The early evening air was warm and the sounds of the city muted.

'Glad to be here?' he asked.

'How can you ask?' she replied, her eyes glowing as she gazed at him.

Emotion turned over in her. It had been hard to leave the *mas*. How could it be otherwise? But knowing that she was not to lose Lycos as well, at least not yet, that she was to have this grace period with him, had eased her taking leave of her beloved home.

And a new resolve had filled her. A new strength. Lycos's words to her had lodged within her, telling her she could make a new life for herself as he had had to do for himself.

She felt her heart clench whenever she thought of what he'd had to endure in his youth, bereft of any kind of love. Her own father had never been unkind to her and had always looked after her until Naomi had got her claws into him. Her mother had been devoted to her. And she to her mother. Their bond had been strong, close and so, so loving. Lycos had never known that, from either parent. Yet he had found the strength in himself to make a new life for himself. And so must she.

Whatever it was to be.

For a moment, dangerous and seductive, as she gazed at him, she felt a longing rise within her.

What if that new life were to be always with Lycos?

The thought hung there in her head, glowing and tempting. Like a golden apple she might reach out and take, and taste.

What if he wants me always to be with him? To make our lives together?

She could see it—as vivid and verdant as if it were real. She and Lycos, back at the *mas*, her home once again. *Their* home together...

I might never lose it. Never lose Lycos.

Emotion tightened around her heart. And a sense of longing rose in her.

She realised he was speaking again. 'After our long

drive shall we just stay local? I know a good little restaurant nearby. Small, but quiet, and the cuisine is superb.'

She smiled. 'That sounds good.'

But then, everything about being with Lycos was good.

As he pulled out his phone to make the reservation, her eyes rested on him, her gaze softening.

Yes, being with Lycos was so very good.

If only it could last for ever...

The restaurant was just as Lycos remembered. They were shown to a table covered with a pristine linen tablecloth and set with silver cutlery and crystal glasses. Ornamented menus were bestowed upon them. As she opened hers, he heard Arielle give a low whistle.

'Lycos, the prices are astronomical!' she exclaimed, sounding perturbed.

'And the cuisine well worth them,' he assured her.

'Yes, but even so—'

He silenced her with a lift of his hand. 'Arielle, I told you. You are here in Paris as my guest. At my expense. For everything.'

He smiled encouragingly. For a moment he saw her hesitate then, as if giving in, she bent her head to study the menu. He was glad she wasn't going to protest again. He wanted to indulge her. And he was glad to do so.

She is not like the women I am used to. She does not expect anything of me, which is exactly why I want to spoil her. Lavish on her the luxury I can so easily afford! I want to see her eyes glow when I give her things. I want to please her.

It warmed him to think that way. Warmed him just to think about her. Just to let his eyes rest on her.

He was not sure why. Oh, that she was so different from the women he'd become used to since he'd made his money, yes, that was one reason. And that he desired her so much. Every long, languorous night at the *mas* had shown him that. That was another reason.

But that was not all.

He let his gaze meet hers, saw hers soften as he did. Saw something in her beautiful blue eyes. Felt it reach out to him.

But how, and why, he did not know. He only knew that he wanted it to be so. Was content for it to be so.

A frown formed on his face, though he veiled it swiftly. There was something he was not content with. She was wearing the blue-sprigged dress again and the loop of blue beads, with no more make-up than the lightest of lip gloss and mascara. Her hair was simply drawn back into a switch. Even with the addition of the shawl he had bought her in Saint-Clément it was an underdressed look that would only do for the provinces. Not for Paris. Not for the circles he moved in.

The frown turned to a glint. Well, that would change tomorrow. For tonight...

'So, what on the menu tempts you?' he prompted.

As for himself, he knew exactly what tempted him. The prospect of fine dining and the pleasures of the night to come.

And all their time in Paris ahead of them.

He would ensure that it was good. For them both.

* * *

'Lycos, I couldn't possibly accept!' Arielle looked at Lycos with troubled eyes.

They were standing in front of one of France's famous fashion houses in the exclusive Faubourg Saint-Honoré and Lycos wanted to go in and buy some clothes for her.

He looked at her straightly. 'Arielle, at the *mas*, in the middle of rural Provence, casual was fine. Here in Paris, it's different. To be chic is *de rigeur*!'

He said the last part lightly, humorously even, but for all that there was an implacable note in his voice. Arielle's troubled expression did not change.

'Well, not for me…' she began. Lycos cut across her.

'Of course for you! Why not?'

'Because I don't move in those circles,' she said flatly.

'Well I do,' he rejoined. 'And I would point out to you that, had your stepmother not got her claws into your father, you would too!'

She shook her head. 'My father was nowhere near as rich as you are, Lycos.'

'But wealthy enough to buy you expensive clothes,' he retorted. 'And now it's me doing so.'

He made to guide her through the impressive double doors with their distinctive, world-famous initials stencilled on them. But still she held back. She felt his grip around her wrist tighten.

'Arielle, here in Paris I socialise, OK? And you are with me, as my guest I told you, so I am covering all expenses! I'll be socialising with you. I'm looking forward to it. Believe me, I can't wait to show you off. Starting tonight. We're dining out with Marc Derenz and his wife. He's my banker, remember, and I'm having my annual review with him at his bank tomorrow. You'll like his wife, by the way. She's English.'

He paused before continuing dryly, holding Arielle's still-troubled gaze, 'She's also a former model and a total knock-out. She'll be looking incredible tonight and I do not want you feeling underdressed in comparison.'

As before, there was humour in his voice but that implacable note remained.

For a moment longer she held back, deeply reluctant to do as Lycos so obviously wanted her to do—to accept him buying her clothes that she could not afford to buy for herself.

But nor could he, once.

She felt her resistance crumble. Lycos had not always been rich. He had come from wretched beginnings and had dreamt of escaping.

And now he has. And if it gives him pleasure to indulge me, to have the wealth now to do so, why should I refuse him?

It's something I can give to him. To let him show me off as he wants to!

So where was the harm in it?

'OK, I give in,' she said. Humour was evident in her voice, and fondness too. She held that image in her head of the neglected, unloved, abused boy in the backstreets of Athens.

For Lycos she would do it. And set aside her qualms.

'Marc, good to see you.' Lycos gave a firm shake of the hand extended to him. He would not call Marc Derenz a friend. He would call no man a friend. That was not his way. But Marc was a man he could trust, indeed did trust, with the investment of a good deal of his money. He was, he knew, a valued client of the prestigious *Banc Derenz*. Marc himself moved in the first circles and was on social terms with all his clients. Including now, Lycos.

Greeting Marc's wife, Lycos drew Arielle forward to introduce her. Tara Derenz might be a former model, and she certainly looked it in the bias-cut silver gown she was wearing, but Arielle was in no way outclassed. No way.

She looked, Lycos knew, stunning.

Superbe! Fantastique! Incroyable!

The French words formed in his head, the only ones to do justice to the vision at his side. The Grecian-style, pale blue gown followed her lovely, curvy figure from breast to ankle. Her lustrous hair was looped up, exposing the nape of her neck, enhancing the height of her cheekbones that were already contoured with skilful shading. Shading that also deepened the colour of her eyes, as mascara lengthened her lashes. Lipstick giving a wondrous sheen and lushness to her mouth.

He'd wondered, briefly, how Tara Derenz would take to a woman who could compete against her, but her smile was warm. So was Arielle's.

'Lycos mentioned you were English,' Arielle said to Tara in English.

'Scots originally,' Tara replied. 'Mackenzie. You sound English too. No French accent at all!'

'My father,' said Arielle. 'But my mother was French.'

'Arielle, what would you like to drink?' Marc asked.

The four of them settled themselves down on the plush

banquette in the very plush cocktail lounge of the extremely plush *Viscari Paris* where they were to dine. Lycos took satisfaction in knowing that Arielle looked perfect for the exclusive setting.

Champagne was mutually agreed on and, as Arielle took a sip of hers, she turned to Lycos with a smile.

'Does it make wine taste better now, do you think, having had the experience of picking the grapes in the first place? Not champagne grapes, of course, but the principle is the same!'

'Picking grapes?' Marc queried, non-plussed.

Lycos turned to him. 'Arielle and I got roped into helping with the grape harvest while staying in Provence.'

Marc's expression was a study. 'Quite a novelty for you,' he said.

'And an enjoyable one,' Lycos said, taking an appreciative mouthful of the superb Viscari house champagne, a unique blend only available at Viscari hotels. 'It was very...' he sought for the right word, '...collaborative. I think we pitched in pretty well, didn't we, Arielle? OK, I didn't do nearly as well as the practised harvesters, but I wasn't too pathetic!'

'You were very good,' Arielle praised him.

'What part of Provence?' Tara Derenz asked with interest. 'Marc is lucky enough to have inherited an original art-deco villa on Cap Saint-Pierre, the last unspoilt *cap* on the Côte d'Azur. But inland is far less spoilt.'

'Quite near Saint-Clément,' Lycos answered. He wanted to change the subject. He did not want to bring up Arielle's lost *mas*. Nor consider why he did not wish to.

'Cap Saint-Pierre,' he mused. 'I must say I've never

been there. I tend to stick to Monaco, Nice and Cannes when I'm at the coast. And, of course, the casinos.'

He made no secret of how he'd acquired his wealth, nor his reputation. Not that that meant anything to Marc Derenz. He had other acquaintances in Paris to whom it signified more. He would meet up with them while he was here, but tonight was for the Derenzes.

'We stick to the *cap*,' Tara said decisively. 'I'm not a fan of cities. Oh, Paris is gorgeous, in its own way. I'll allow that. But when we married we made Versailles our base. Though Marc keeps a *pied-à-terre* handy over the bank.'

'Versailles sounds, well, palatial!' Arielle smiled.

'It is. And the palace grounds are ideal for pushchairs!' responded Tara.

Lycos heard Arielle enquire after the occupants of the pushchairs and was glad to realise she and Marc's wife seemed to be hitting it off. They went on chatting. An easy conversation switching in and out of French and English. He turned to Marc to ask him something about the current French political scene. Menus were bestowed upon them. Choices made, champagne consumed, they made their way into the Viscari's Michelin-starred restaurant to take their table. The evening was going well and Lycos was glad.

His eyes were still feasting on Arielle. How fantastic she looked. *En grande tenue* indeed. Effortlessly holding her own in these luxury surroundings. She was relaxed and he was glad for that too.

He realised he was also relaxed. And enjoying himself. The Derenzes might be an established married couple, but he and Arielle were—

Were what?

He paused inwardly a moment, searching for the *bon mot*.

At ease with each other. That's what we are.

It was a strange thought and he wondered why it should be so. He was not unused to female company after all.

But never before have I spent so much time, continuous time, with one single female. Those weeks at the mas, *just being together. Living together.*

At ease together.

Even as he thought it, memories flashed. 'Ease' had not been there between them at first—the very opposite.

The first time he'd set eyes on her, in that faded dressing gown, in the courtyard of *Mas Delfine*.

Staring at me as if I were the demon king arriving to dispossess her. Come to take her home from her.

He shook the accusation away. Not only was it not true, it had been her father who was to blame, not him, for her loss. But now he was not taking from Arielle. He was giving.

His eyes rested on her again, warm and appreciative. How stunning she looked in the gown he'd bought her. That was only one of their purchases today and more would follow. He would buy jewellery for her too and lavish his lifestyle on her. Just as he was doing this evening and would do throughout their stay in Paris.

I want to please her, to indulge her, because she is worth it to me. She's valuable. She's...

Another word formed in his head.

Precious.

It hung there a moment, like a pearl, and something

moved within him. Something he did not recognise, but which kept his gaze on her arrested. Then Marc made some remark, requiring his response and the moment was gone. But as Arielle turned her head to him, her beautiful eyes smiling and meeting his for a moment, he heard the echo of that word again.

Precious.

And that strange, elusive, unrecognised emotion that came with it echoed too.

CHAPTER NINE

ARIELLE GAZED AT the city of Paris from the topmost viewing platform of the Eiffel Tower, Lycos beside her, his arm around her waist. It was only one of the many sights of the city she'd seen with him. Some she had already known from childhood visits with her mother, but even those she revelled in again, seeing them afresh with Lycos. But then Lycos could have taken her on a tour of the sewers—a popular if eclectic tourist attraction—and she would have wanted to go.

Anywhere he wants. Anywhere at all.

While he wanted her to go with him. Be with him.

She felt an ache pluck at her that she sought to dismiss.

How long do I have with him?

She didn't know. She didn't even know how long he wanted to stay in Paris. The days had been full of sightseeing, the evenings with dining out at fabulous restaurants. And several times Lycos had taken her to the theatre, to the opera and to a concert to hear a world-famous pianist, one of her very favourites, give a heart-stopping concert performance. Tickets had been gold-dust, but somehow Lycos had obtained them, producing them with a flourish that had made her exclaim with thrilled disbelief.

As well as the city's sights they'd been out to Versailles, not just to tour the grand palace, but to dine with the Derenzes again at their elegant, nineteenth-century townhouse. They had been warmly welcomed. Tara had taken her up to the nursery floor to make the acquaintance of their two young children.

Arielle had taken to Tara from the off, knowing they might have become friends, except that there would be no opportunity.

Soon I will be in England making my new life there, whatever it is to be, and this time here, in Paris, will be gone. As my life at the mas *will be gone.*

And her time with Lycos…

Her thoughts sheered away. She must not let them in, nor the emotions that went with them. Emotions she must not have, because there could be no purpose to them, except to cause her pain. She must take this time with Lycos only for what it was.

That it will not last. That the moment will come when he is done with Paris. Done with me. Then my time with him will end, as my time at the mas *has ended.*

Even with Lycos's arm around her, she felt pain clench.

My home and Lycos. I must bear the loss of both.

Because what else could there be?

'Lycos! *Chérie—*'

The woman greeting him as he and Arielle made their way into the VIP section at the fashionable racecourse on the outskirts of Paris bestowed a kiss on his cheek that lasted more than was socially necessary, enveloping him in a cloud of heavy perfume.

'Natalie,' he returned. Lycos shook hands with the man next to her. He was not Natalie's husband, but he was rich, hence Natalie's presence in his life. Paul Ronsard was in finance, with fingers in many pies, all of which were highly lucrative. His amusements, other than expensive mistresses, were gambling and horse racing. The former was how Lycos knew him, the latter was why he and Arielle were spending the afternoon here.

He saw Paul's eyes go to Arielle. She was looking stunning in another newly-bought outfit, a cerulean-blue slub silk suit with a cinched waist and contrasting lapels. Her hair was up and adorned by a confection that was half fascinator, half stylish hat, with a wisp of veiling that drew attention to her vivid blue eyes.

Though Lycos revelled in the fact that Arielle looked so stunning, there was something about Paul's glance he did not care for. It was…assessing.

But he made the introduction civilly, aware, too, that Natalie was glancing at Arielle in a far from friendly fashion. But then that was not surprising. Natalie was well into her thirties now and Arielle's youthful freshness would not be a welcome comparison. Women like Natalie had a limited shelf-life. They had to make the most of it while it lasted. Make the most of being favoured by rich men.

He snapped his mind away, Arielle was not of that sisterhood and to even think of it was to insult her. The likes of Natalie expected the men in their lives to lavish their money on them.

That was not how it was for Arielle and himself. She expected nothing, asked for nothing, but he gave it to her anyway.

I buy beautiful clothes for her because I want to show off her beauty. To herself as well as to me, and to the world. I am showing her Paris to please her. So she can enjoy herself. Just as I took her to that concert that so thrilled her!

And now he wanted her to enjoy today, as well. He'd asked her if she cared for horse racing, but all she'd said was that she'd never been. So hopefully the novelty of it would engage her. He broadened his introduction of her to the others in Paul's party, some of whom were already known to him. They all came with expensively dressed, highly ornamental female companions, of Natalie's ilk. The kind he himself used to be involved with.

Arielle was nothing like them.

Nor were his feelings about her.

He touched her wrist lightly, but reassuringly. She had a reserved air about her and he wanted her to relax, to enjoy this afternoon at the races. She gave a faint smile as he introduced her, but did not join in the general conversation much. Lycos hoped she was not feeling shy.

But she wasn't shy with the Derenzes. She was quite at ease with them.

Perhaps that had been because Tara Derenz was English or because there'd only been one other couple, rather than a whole group of people in the party. Whatever the reason, her quietness now was noticeable. But then very few remarks, if any, were addressed to her directly. He noticed, with a flicker of realisation, that the women present were not often directly addressed either. Their contributions to the conversation were usually giving compliments to the men, or giving them smiles of approval and little laughs of appreciation, or asking wide-eyed questions for them to explain or confirm something they'd remarked on.

He found himself wondering why he was noticing it.

Then he shook the idea from him. Drinks were being served. Lycos took one for Arielle and himself. Food would be served later, though he and Arielle had had a late brunch earlier on before setting off for the racecourse.

He hadn't driven himself. He kept his car valet-parked whenever he was in Paris and stuck to taxis for ease and convenience, and to avoid limitations on alcohol. He took a sip now from his martini, enjoying its kick. Arielle had requested a soft drink and was stirring the ice with a cocktail stick, as though giving herself something to do.

The racing had started, but no one in their party was paying any attention. Initial conversation focussed on racing in general, but then veered off to focus instead on the exchange of updates with each other about recent social events in a variety of geographical locations. Since he and Arielle had not been to any of the events, Lycos did not contribute. Then one member of the party addressed him, changing the subject.

'So, when do we get to see you back in action, Lycos? Can we get something going while you're in Paris? It would need to be a private party, now that gaming clubs are coming under fire.'

'If you like,' Lycos said. He wasn't particularly keen, but then nor did he object. He might not need to play cards any longer, but he liked to keep his hand in. Keep his skill honed.

'Good, I'll get something set up,' came the reply. 'It will be good to see the Wolf back on the prowl! The *on dit* from the Riviera where you last went hunting was that you badly mauled a bulldog Englishman who baited you but was not a gracious loser. You took a villa off him, so I heard, after you'd cleaned him out!'

At his side, Lycos felt Arielle freeze.

'Did I?' He shrugged one indifferent shoulder. 'No doubt he deserved it.'

'In your book they all deserve it! Hubris for taking you on.'

'They know what they're doing,' Lycos replied shortly. He glanced briefly at Arielle, wanting to move her away. Her fingers were gripped tightly around her glass. 'Would you like to see something of the racing?' he asked her. 'There's another race about to start.'

She nodded and he guided her away towards the rails at the edge of the course. The horses lined up as the Tannoy announced the runners and riders. Lycos procured a race card from a steward and held it so they could both read it.

'I'm sorry you heard that remark about your stepbrother,' he said.

'It doesn't matter,' she said quickly. 'It wasn't news to me after all.' She looked at him. 'Thank you for not telling them about *Mas Delfine*.'

'I wouldn't dream of it,' Lycos assured her.

She was still looking at him. 'Did that man say he was inviting you to some kind of gambling session?'

'A private party, yes. Unless he can find a gaming club that is still operating.'

Arielle frowned. Lycos explained.

'Paris banned casinos in the nineteenth century,' he said. 'The authorities were concerned that workers would waste their wages. There are no casinos within a hundred kilometres of the city. A few gaming clubs were permitted, but even those are being banned. It's a controversial issue.'

'You're on the side of the casinos and clubs, I take it?' Arielle's voice was expressionless. It made Lycos frown.

'Arielle, I no longer rely on gambling to make money. Didn't our dinner with Marc Derenz demonstrate that?' He paused a moment. He wanted her to understand this. 'I'm not an addict, Arielle. Nor am I a professional. That's a whole different ball game, with international rankings, competitions and so on. Gambling to me was, and still is, simply a way of making money by using skills I happen to possess and which I have honed to a high degree by my own experience. If I'd been good at any other way of making money, I'd have followed that. Gambling, cards, is just a means to an end, that's all. It's not important to me for its own sake.'

She looked at him. Her expression was strange. 'Do you mean that, Lycos?' she asked.

'Yes,' he said. 'Why do you ask?'

'Because today is the first time I've come face to face with it, I suppose. These people here, you seem to know them because of gambling. It's...it's a side of you I haven't seen till now.'

He made to speak, but the thunder of approaching

hooves made it impossible. For a handful of seconds there was nothing but the sight of the horses pounding past, a rush of air and the noise of drumming hooves.

When all that subsided, the moment was gone and he realised that Paul was approaching them, together with Natalie and the others in the party.

'My horse is running next,' Paul announced. He indicated a name on the list for the next race on the card. 'Wish me luck. I've placed a large bet on it. Plus the prize money is handsome. My trainer and jockey know they need to win for me.'

The announcement of the results of the race that had just gone by were made as the horses for the next race lined up.

Lycos made a polite show of interest but it was all over in minutes and Paul's horse was unplaced.

'Well, he's enjoyed his last helping of oats,' Paul said, tearing up his betting slip and dropping the shards on the ground.

'What's going to happen to him?' Arielle's voice was sharp.

Paul cast her a cynical glance. 'He'll be destroyed. I don't keep horses that don't earn their keep. This race was his last chance. He cost me a lot of money in the bet I placed. Plus he won me no prize money.'

'You're going to kill him because he's lost you money?' Arielle protested.

'That, *mademoiselle*, is the name of the game,' Paul replied patronisingly.

Lycos felt Arielle clutch his sleeve as she turned to him.

'Lycos, please, offer to buy him!'

Arielle then turned to Paul.

'Or you could just give him to Lycos for free. After all, it would save you the vet fees for putting him down!' she said witheringly.

Paul gave a short laugh. 'Well, Lycos. Are you going to indulge your animal-loving lady? Start a rescue centre for endangered racehorses?' His words were mocking.

Lycos ignored him. He peeled Arielle's hand off his sleeve. 'It isn't practical,' he told her.

She stared at him.

'Arielle, no.' His voice was flat. 'It's out of the question.'

For a moment she just went on staring at him. Then, abruptly, her gaze dropped and she looked away out over the now-deserted racecourse. Another race was being lined up, but that was of no interest to Paul, who had no money in it, and he ushered his party back to their table. A cold collation had been set out and more champagne provided.

'Commiserations instead of congratulations,' Paul intoned ponderously. 'Ah well, I have more horses to race another time.'

'And kill if they lose,' Lycos heard Arielle mutter, *sotto voce*. He could hear the anger in her voice. The outrage.

It irritated him.

And out of nowhere, the afternoon had ceased to be enjoyable.

Arielle perched on the edge of the bed in their hotel room, careful not to crease her evening gown. She heard the sound of the shower from the bathroom where Lycos was freshening up for the evening ahead—the private party dedicated to gaming that had been discussed at the racecourse a few days ago. She wasn't looking forward to it. Presumably, the same people who'd been at the races, or others like them, would be there tonight as well.

She'd disliked the lot of them. The men were repellent, especially that vile man who was going to kill an innocent horse for losing and the others who were self-satisfied and condescending. The women were clearly there as trophies for their looks alone.

A sudden chill went through her.

Is that how Lycos sees me?

She shook the acid thought from her head, rejecting it. She wasn't just some kind of trophy to Lycos any more than the stunning Tara was to her husband.

She was glad that Lycos found her beautiful, and she was honest enough to admit in return how his looks could make her melt with a single glance, but that wasn't all there was between them. There was so much more.

I like being with him. I like his company. It's enjoyable to be with him and spend time with him.

Though very different from the peace of their weeks at the *mas*, this fortnight in Paris had been wonderful. Her disquiet at Lycos buying her beautiful clothes had eased, and she was getting all too used to fine dining and high living.

But it was not that that she valued. Of course not. It was being with Lycos. They could have been staying in a modest *pension*, eating in cheap cafes and bars, seeing Paris on a budget, and she'd have been just as happy. Just as content.

Until he finishes with me.

The familiar clenching of her heart came. The one that always came when she thought about the future with Lycos.

The absence of it...

They were living day by day, as they had at the *mas*. Taking each day as it came, with no discussion as to how long this time they were having together would last.

Sometimes she desperately wanted to ask him what she meant to him. But she never dared.

An old saying of her mother's came into her head. Something about how, in love, there was always one who kissed and one who merely offered the cheek to be kissed.

Is that Lycos and me? With me doing the kissing and Lycos just letting me?

But it had been he who'd made clear to her his desire for her.

Yes, but I have no guarantee how long that will last.

Oh, it was burning fiercely still, his desire for her. Every passionate night in his arms told her that. But would it not burn itself out one day? For him at least...

And for me? Will it burn out for me?

Desire and everything else he meant to her. But what was that? What did Lycos mean to her?

The questions went round in her head and she did not know the answer to any of them. Maybe, she sighed inwardly, Lycos was right just to live as they were doing—taking each day as it came.

Including this evening, which she was not looking forward to. She got to her feet, heading to the dressing table. The shower had cut out and Lycos would be emerging any moment, getting himself dressed in his tuxedo, setting out with her. She gazed at her reflection in the mirror. She was in full make-up with hair up-styled elaborately. Her evening gown, yet another one that Lycos had bought for her that morning, was in *eau-de-nil* silk with a low cut draped decolletage. Exquisitely beautiful, but it had been terrifyingly expensive.

He'd insisted on adding a necklace as well, a diamond drop, with matching drop earrings. She hadn't wanted him to. It made her uneasy. And even though she told herself, as she had when he'd first wanted to buy her expensive clothes, that she was doing it to please him by wearing something so valuable so that he could triumph over memories of his miserable, impoverished childhood, it did not assuage her unease.

I'm getting too used to this luxury lifestyle with him.

It was a disturbing thought.

Even if, painfully rather than disturbingly, she knew it could not and would not last.

The mas *has gone and cannot last for ever.*

Nor me in Lycos's life...

She reached for her lipstick, a heaviness in her heart. She had lost her beloved home and soon, all too soon, she would lose Lycos. And any foolish dreams she might weave that there could be a future with Lycos, making their home together at the *mas*, were surely just that—dreams.

It could never happen.

CHAPTER TEN

Lycos's expression was shuttered. His adrenaline levels were slightly raised, but not from excitement. The very reverse. He knew exactly what mental state he was entering as he walked with Arielle at his side into the grand townhouse, windows lit up for the party already underway, in an elegant terrace off the Place de l'étoile in a wealthy Right Bank *arrondissement*.

Did he regret accepting the invitation for tonight? Arielle had been wary about just what was involved. But she'd agreed, all the same, and Lycos got the impression she was curious about this side of his life. The one that was so familiar to him.

It's the life I've been leading with Arielle that is unfamiliar to me.

Peaceful days at the *mas*, one following another in bucolic ease. And the days here in Paris sightseeing, visiting art galleries and museums, going to classical music concerts and the opera—Arielle was expanding his own experiences.

Tonight, it was his turn to show her his world.

Thoughts flickered as he made his way forward, greeting those he knew. Paul Ronsard would not be here this evening as he was in London on business. Lycos was glad, for Arielle's sake. That exchange over the horse had obviously upset her.

But the guests here tonight, even if not known personally to him, were all of a similar kind. Drawn together for one reason only—to gamble. It was the world he knew and had made his own.

But is it still?

He'd told Arielle that gambling was no longer the way he made his money. That he continued with it only to keep his skills honed. And that was why he was here tonight. Arielle, at his side, was looking stunning again in a couture gown, her throat adorned with a diamond necklace. Tonight, she would witness the way in which he had come to be able to afford to buy such lavish gifts for her.

He moved on through the gathering guests, guiding Arielle forward at his side.

Arielle smiled politely and took a canape. She was making minimal contribution to whatever conversation was taking place. Some of the people in their group were familiar from that race day she hadn't enjoyed and all were of the same type. Opulent, self-congratulatory, over-pleased with themselves, men and women both. The latter visibly on display.

Does Lycos really like these people?

She couldn't tell. His expression was shuttered and there was a detachment about him that gave him an air of reserve. She realised he'd stopped meeting her eyes, seemed to have withdrawn into himself. Nor was he drinking alcohol, she noticed. Only bottled water, sparkling and flavourless.

He's keeping his mind clear. Sharp. He can risk no impairment of mental function.

She felt a knot of tension tighten within her. Soon, she supposed, the gaming would begin. For Lycos's sake she would endure it.

It's important to him. Gambling is not casual self-indulgence to him. It's his skill, his ability, his achievement. It was the ladder that took him out of poverty. Out of that sad, unhappy childhood. That let him make something of his life. That has given him the means to live life as wealth makes possible.

And who was she to be hypocritical about wealth? Had Naomi not married her father she herself would be wealthy, not just scraping by on the modest sum he'd made over to her as a student. Oh, she'd have been nowhere near Lycos's league, but she'd have had enough to allow her to do what she liked with her life. Not to have to work to earn a living, but be able to look after her beloved *mas*. To follow her music and have a pleasant, financially carefree life. Her father had made his money through shrewd property investment. Lycos had made his through his skill at cards. He won from those who, like all those here tonight, could easily afford to lose. If they pitted their wits against the Wolf *and* came off the worse for it, so what?

She felt a faint touch on her bare arm.

'Arielle?' Lycos was addressing her. His voice was polite, his tone detached.

She realised he was making a move and so were others.

Docilely she went with him. Lycos had already told her on the way here that she was welcome in the card room, but must remain quiet, standing away from the tables.

'I have to remain entirely focussed. There will be breaks from time to time, but during play there must be no distractions. You will have to leave me entirely alone. Do you understand?'

She'd nodded. She had no intention of getting involved in the slightest.

He's welcome to fleece anyone here! I couldn't care less!

Would he do so tonight? It seemed likely, according to his reputation. He was, after all, the Wolf and those who played against him did so of their own choice.

At their own risk.

Just as I am with him at my own risk.

The thought was in her head before she could stop it.

But what was it she was risking? And what might she lose?

She headed upstairs, Lycos at her side, unwilling to answer either question.

Lycos sat at the table he'd selected. The world had disappeared. All that existed were the cards displayed in his hand and the calculations running through his head. He paid little attention to the other players. Only to what cards they played, what money they staked and when. He was entirely focussed on the progress of the game. His mind was in a flow state, everything else obliterated from consciousness except that necessary to move the state of play to where he wanted it to go. Adapting his decisions to what each new card, his or his opponents', denoted.

Emotion, of any kind, was entirely absent. His play was remorseless. His face expressionless.

The Wolf was here to win.

Arielle suppressed an inner sigh. She could make no sense of what was happening. At first, she'd been warily curious to see what was involved, but it had not taken long to realise that a game in which she had no idea what the rules of play were would be impossible to follow. Watching the players push their chips forward was unnerving, given their cash value, but she had no idea why they were making the stakes they were making. She certainly had no idea at all what Lycos was doing, or why. She could tell nothing about him whatsoever. His expression was entirely blank. Nothing showed in his face, eyes or body language.

Players had 'tells', so watching the occasional movie featuring gambling had told her, but that didn't seem to apply to Lycos.

It's like watching a robot.

He showed nothing, whether the pile of chips that were his rose or fell.

That wasn't so with all of the players though. Some players, at the end of a game, showed satisfaction or chagrin. When a game ended, they remarked to each other and discussed what had happened. Lycos kept silent. No one tried to talk to him or engage him. Until the next game started, he simply took a used pack of cards and shuffled it mechanically to occupy his hands. His face remained expressionless, his eyes blank, while he took an occasional sip of water from the glass in front of him. She did not try and engage him either. He made no move to turn to her, talk to her, or even to acknowledge her existence.

She found it chilling.

On impulse, she slipped from the room. The atmosphere in there was oppressive. Everyone there simply wanted to make money. To win, to triumph, to beat their opponents, to outdo them. Including, presumably, Lycos.

It was a side of him she'd never seen and she found it unnerving.

Out on the landing she hesitated for a moment, then scooped up the long skirt of her gown and made her way up the next set of stairs. The bathrooms set aside for guests were up here, so she recalled someone mentioning. Maybe she could lurk up there until Lycos called it quits.

When would he, she wondered?

If I really get bored and I can't stand it, I'll head back to the hotel in a taxi and just text him to let him know that I've gone.

She doubted he would notice or even realise she wasn't in the card room any longer.

A door standing ajar on the deserted upper floor indicated that it was a bathroom and she approached it. As she did, she heard a voice speaking and paused. It was coming from the bathroom. She didn't want to eavesdrop, but had no choice.

'I know and I don't want to do it! I know how risky it

is! But I'm going to, all the same. I've got to try! It's all I can think of. It's our only chance.'

She could half see the speaker, his body in profile, holding a mobile phone to his ear. He fell silent a moment, then spoke again, sounding impatient. Stressed.

'There's no point saying that! I know what I'm doing. Look, I have to go.'

She saw him disconnect the call and then stride out of the bathroom. His expression was steely and tension radiated from him. As he saw Arielle he halted abruptly. He was a young man, in his early twenties she judged. He was good-looking and his French, she realised, had been distinctly upper-class.

'Excuse me,' he said, sounding curt as he skirted around her to head downstairs with a rapid gait.

She thought no more about it as she headed into the plush bathroom. Deliberately she dallied in there, retouching her lipstick, re-spritzing her perfume and then availing herself of a basket of necessities on the vanity unit. She searched through a tiny sewing kit to extract a couple of safety pins. She hoicked up her decolletage, which she fancied was too low, and fastened it discreetly. Eventually she could delay no longer.

Would Lycos still be immersed in his card game?

Probably.

At least she didn't have to worry about him losing. *After all, he was the Wolf*, she thought sardonically. And anyway, with his wealth he could presumably shrug off any losses.

She frowned. It couldn't always have been like that.

When he was young and trying to make his fortune, it must have been nerve-wracking for him.

The words of that young man on the phone just now came back to her. In his tone, anxiety warring with determination.

Had Lycos once been like that? Needing to win. Fearing to lose.

Well, that didn't apply any longer. Reluctantly she headed downstairs again, and slipped into the card room where Lycos was playing. Someone had already said it was the room with the deepest play. Just right for the Wolf.

He was still there, at the same table. Players came to him, it seemed, for now there were fresh faces around him.

Do they not care about losing to him, which is what seems likely to happen?

Presumably not. Everyone here was rich and was gambling for pleasure. They could afford to lose to Lycos. What they seemed to want, she'd seen, was to have played against him whether they won or lost.

Two new players took their places. One of them was apparently known to Lycos who afforded him the slightest nod and a brief greeting but nothing more. Fresh decks of cards were being set down and the two other players were arranging their chips. As for Lycos, he sat motionless. Arielle wondered whether to approach him, but refrained, mindful of his admonition not to distract him.

Another player joined the table, taking the place opposite Lycos, setting down his chips with an air of studied deliberation. Arielle recognised him. It was the young man who'd been on the phone upstairs. He sat back in his chair, one hand resting on the baize, a gold signet ring with an aristocratic crest on it, glinted in the light. He seemed to give off an air of unconcern but Arielle frowned. The unconcern seemed forced. Or was it, considering who he was playing against, mere bravado? Arrogance even?

A voice beside her spoke as she stood near the wall.

'His father's a *vicomte*,' the woman, also an observer, murmured. 'Handsome, isn't he? And he knows it! He's brave to choose the Wolf's table though!' She gave a low laugh and moved away towards the bar that occupied one side of the room.

Arielle leant back against the wall behind Lycos. Play started at his table. The cards were dealt and drawn. Chips were moved about. She couldn't tell what was happening. The hush and palpable concentration in the room oppressed her. Play continued at several tables and she suppressed a yawn.

Her eyes started to glaze.

Lycos watched as the player opposite him hesitated then moved more chips forward. He knew why and he knew what his own reaction would be whatever decision was made next. But he also knew what the player's next decision would be and moments later it was confirmed. More of the player's chips were pushed forward.

It was a stupid move because Lycos knew what cards he was likely to be holding and that the chances of improving them by his next draw were not good. But then he wasn't a skilful player. He made rash, unwise decisions.

The light glinted off his crested signet ring and the 'de' in front of his name when introductions had been made told Lycos what he was. Some cocky aristocratic sprig, playing way out of his league. He would lose. And badly.

Play continued. Lycos continued to win.

The way the Wolf always did.

Arielle edged over to the bar set up at the far side of the room. She didn't want any alcohol, but her throat was dry. Asking for a flavoured tonic water, she perched on a bar stool. The room was a lot emptier now than it had been earlier. Observers had wandered off and two of the card tables were deserted. Now, maybe, she thought, only the hard-core gamblers remained. She sipped her tonic water, watching Lycos's table. After a while one of his opponents folded and left the table. The second was, it seemed to her, playing half-heartedly. The third, the young man, the *vicomte's* son, was betting heavily.

Very heavily.

Arielle started to frown. There was something else different about him now. He was no longer unconcernedly leant back, resting his signet-ring fingered hand casually on the baize. In fact, he wasn't looking unconcerned at all.

His jaw was taut, mouth compressed, his face pale and, in his cheek, Arielle could see a tic working. Tension sat across his shoulders. His movements, as he drew cards or moved chips forward, were jerky.

He was losing. She could see that plainly enough. And his chips were going only in one direction. Towards his opponent. The Wolf.

Her eyes went to Lycos. His face was still expressionless, unreadable. From time to time his blank gaze rested on the young man, then returned to his own hand. The other players' chips continued to dwindle. Arielle could see a new emotion show on the younger player's face. Saw it and saw too that his movements were no longer just hesitant. His hands were trembling.

And in his face, and in his eyes, was a look of disbelief.

And something more...

Desperation.

Lycos set down his hand.

To his left the other player exclaimed with a pungent oath and displayed his own hand. Strong, but not enough to beat the Wolf.

Lycos's eyes went to the player opposite. The cocky aristocratic sprig with whom he'd all but wiped the floor. He waited expectantly. For a moment, the young man hesitated, then showed his cards. Lycos said nothing, only gathered the chips in play towards himself. The player to his left got to his feet.

'Enough. The Wolf wins. Again. Damn him!'

Lycos said nothing, only gave a curt nod as the man left the table. His eyes rested on the remaining player.

'Well?' His voice was expressionless.

For a moment there was silence. He could see the young man's face work. Then his chin went up defiantly.

'I don't quit, *m'sieu*,' he said. His voice was gritted.

'As you wish,' said Lycos. His glance dropped to the meagre pile of chips still at the young man's side. 'Are you good for credit?'

Something flashed in the young man's eyes, as though he'd been insulted.

'*D'accord*,' he said.

Lycos gave another curt nod. 'Very well.'

He reached for a new pack of cards.

Arielle lurched to her feet, abandoning her drink. Rapidly she went up to Lycos.

He had started to deal. Her hand went to his shoulder.

'Lycos, no—'

Her voice was low. Insistent.

He stilled. He did not turn, or look at her.

'*Laisse moi*—'

It was not said loudly, and it might have been a robot speaking, but still she recoiled as if he had struck her. Then she leant forward, voice urgent.

'Lycos, for God's sake. Don't play him again! Can't you see—'

His head snapped round. His eyes were like a basilisk's. He gave her a murderous look.

For one endless moment she held that basilisk stare. Then she dragged her gaze across the table. To the young man. He was scarcely more than a boy.

'Don't play,' she said directly to him. 'Accept your losses and go home.'

She got no answer. Instead, someone took her arm and drew her away. It was the player who had just lost to Lycos and had accepted his losses with a pungent oath.

'Leave them,' he said. 'There's nothing you can do. The boy has to learn.' His voice came sardonic. 'And believe me, the Wolf will teach him.'

Arielle's eyes flared. 'But he's terrified! Can't you see it? He's way out of his depth, and—'

'And it is not your business, or the Wolf's.' He gave a shrug. 'His father's a *vicomte*. He can stand the loss.'

'Then why is he so terrified?'

The man shrugged again. 'Loss of face,' he said. 'But he was a fool to join the table. Anyone could have told him that. Take my advice. Let this play out to the end. You can't stop it anyway. Not if Lycos is willing to accept vowels—the kid's IOU. Who knows...' he gave a rough laugh, '...the Wolf might end the night the owner of an aristocrat's *château*!'

He walked away, leaving the room on a heavy tread. The room was all but deserted now. No other tables were in play.

Silently, Arielle went back to her place by the wall, behind Lycos. She felt sick. Sick and angry. Angry like the way she'd felt at the racecourse when that vile man had said he was killing his horse because it hadn't made him any money.

Sick like the way she'd felt when Lycos had turned up at the *mas* and told her that he'd won it in a game of cards.

And now—

With heart thudding, she watched the game unfold until its inevitable conclusion.

Lycos crossed to the bar. The evening was finished. He ordered a martini and knocked it back in one. Then he glanced around. He frowned. Arielle had disappeared. His frown deepened. He had not meant to shut her down like that, but he had warned her that she must not interrupt him.

Let alone for such a reason.

His mouth curled. In his jacket pocket was a signed and witnessed IOU, the signature a shaky scrawl. Of the *vicomte's* gilded son there was no sign. Off to lick his wounded ego no doubt.

He pushed back his empty martini glass. Wherever Arielle had got to, she would find him ready to go home. Chips cashed, winnings ready to bank.

Time to celebrate. And he knew just how he would do so. Had it not been for years of rigid self-discipline Arielle tonight would have been a fatal distraction. But now, now she could distract him all she liked. He would apologise for snapping at her. They would get back to the hotel and order room service. He was hungry now for more than Arielle. And then for dessert... Well, the night was long and dessert could take a long, long time to feast on...

He left the room, heading downstairs. Arielle must have gone down already.

Arielle leant against the wall outside the bathroom. The door was closed shut, but she could hear the sound of retching. She knew who it was, she had followed him upstairs. He had held it together until Lycos had left the table. Then he had walked, like a zombie, white-faced, from the room.

The sound of retching ended and she heard water running. She backed away, down to the dimly lit end of the corridor, out of sight. He would not want his misery witnessed.

Only when she heard footsteps heading down did she move. On heavy tread she made her way downstairs to the entrance hall.

She saw Lycos waiting there.

His expression as she came up to him was warm.

But hers was like stone.

Lycos sat back in the taxi, Arielle beside him. She was looking out of the window, drawn a little apart from him and very quiet. He assumed she was tired. As for himself, he knew this state of mind too. Mentally exhausted, half still fully focussed, half detached. It took him a while to come down from the mental state he needed to be in to follow the play and fall of the cards. He sat back musing absently, eyes unseeing, as the Paris traffic went past at this late hour. The last time he'd played had been when he'd taken down Gerald Maitland. Taken his money and his *mas* and then driven up the Rhône valley through the night.

It had proved a fateful journey. And a fateful win.

It brought Arielle into my life.

His head turned slightly, eyes half-open. She sat, face averted, in half profile. On impulse he reached for her hand, folding his around it. It felt cold to his touch. Inert.

Arielle waited until they were back in their room at the hotel. Her head was aching, a tight band around it. She made for the bathroom.

'I need a shower,' she said. She knew her voice sounded strained, but she also knew why. She barely looked at Lycos.

He nodded. 'I'll get on to room service. What would you like?'

'Oh...whatever,' she managed to say. She shut the bathroom door, wanting only privacy.

Her mind was in turmoil, yet blank at the same time. For a moment she stared at herself in the mirror over the vanity. She looked like a stranger. Alien.

But then so had Lycos, sitting at that card table.

In her head she heard his low, bitten out words when she'd tried to intervene in his demolition of that hapless boy.

'Laisse moi!'

She inhaled a sharp breath, which stabbed her as if a knife. Face contorting, with a sudden movement, she started to strip off her finery. Dress hooked on the back of the door, necklace with its pendent diamond dropped into the toiletries' basket. She reached for her face cleanser and removed all of her make-up. When she'd finished her face looked bare.

And bleak.

Discarding her undies, she stepped into the shower, turning the water on full. Drenching her body. Washing something away.

Something she needed to wash away.

Lycos opened the door to room service. He was barefoot and dressed in his bathrobe, feeling a lot more comfortable out of his tux. Mentally he had pretty much come back down from his detached, elevated state. He was hungry for food. And for Arielle. He stood aside while the waiter set out the dishes and then left the room. He heard the shower cut out and Arielle emerged. Like him, she was dressed in a bathrobe. Her face was clear of make-up and her hair had been brushed out. His face lit up with a smile and he held her chair at the table for her.

'I've gone Italian,' he announced. 'I hope that appeals?'

She nodded, taking her place. He looked at her. She seemed different but he wasn't quite sure how.

'Are you OK?' he asked, concerned.

She pressed her lips a moment. 'Headache,' she said.

'You should eat something. This evening was not relaxing.'

'No,' she agreed. She didn't meet his eyes.

Leaving the pasta carbonara to stay warm in its covered tureen, Lycos raised his glass. He'd ordered a robust Italian red wine to go with the pasta.

'Well, here's to it being over and to us relaxing. *Santé!*' he toasted.

She did not answer him, but she picked up her wine glass and took a draught. As she set back the glass, so did he.

'Tomorrow,' he announced, 'we'll have the day entirely to ourselves. And the evening. No more socialising.' He looked at her, his expression quizzical. 'And no more gaming parties.'

She looked at him now, across the table. 'Lycos, why do you still gamble? You don't need the money any more.'

He met her eyes. They were troubled. Questioning.

'No, I don't,' he agreed. 'But as I've told you, I don't want to lose my edge. It's the one skill I have.'

'But you don't need it any more.'

He looked at her and chose his words carefully, so she would understand.

'Tell me something. You trained as a musician. You studied it for three years. It's your skill. If someone asked you why you still play the piano, even though you don't make a living out of it, what would you tell them?'

She shook her head. 'It's not the same.'

'Why not?'

She didn't answer. He let it be. He was hungry and served up the pasta, getting stuck in with gusto. Arielle ate too, but less hungrily. There was still that different air about her. She seemed withdrawn, troubled.

He didn't want that feeling to be there.

Clearing his dish, he set down his fork. Looked across at her.

'Arielle, I owe you an apology. And I give it to you freely. I'd hoped I'd given you fair warning that you must not interrupt or distract me during play.' He paused, looking directly at her. She wasn't meeting his eyes.

'Is that why you're upset with me?' he said.

She still didn't look at him, but she set down her fork.

'No,' she said. Her voice was low. 'It was because of that boy. That boy I tried to stop you playing with!'

'Boy?' he said blankly.

Her eyes flashed. 'Yes, boy! Because that's all he was, Lycos! Barely of a legal age to gamble! You demolished him! You totally demolished him! How much did he lose in the end? You made him sign some kind of IOU on top of taking everything else he had! His hand shook when he signed it. I saw it!'

Lycos sat back. His face had shuttered.

'He knew what he was getting into. There were other tables he could have joined, where the play was not so deep. And he would not have had to face playing me. He *chose* to do so, Arielle. And that is *not* my responsibility! I have a well-known reputation and those who take it into their heads to challenge me do so at their own risk! If some spoilt rich kid wants to boast that he played against the Wolf, and got wiped out instead, that's his problem!'

His voice rose slightly.

'I've seen types like him all my life. Arrogant, conceited, flaunting their money, taking it for granted, wasting it on anything they want to waste it on, including their gaming losses. So what makes that pampered kid tonight any different from your stepbrother? Do you bleed over him being taken to the cleaners by the Wolf? No, you don't. So don't bleed over some wet-behind-the-ears idiot who fancied himself playing against me and got taught a life-long lesson for his pains. Not that it will cost him anything!'

His voice twisted derisively.

'He'll just dip into his trust fund, that's all. Or trot to his doting *papa*, the *vicomte*, to pay his debt for him! All that's injured is his pride as he slinks off with his tail between his legs!'

'Lycos, he looked sick and was white as a sheet. And I heard him throwing up afterwards, in the bathroom.'

He shrugged angrily. 'So what? He was probably liquored up.'

'He was sick with fear. He looked terrified as he left the room. And even before he joined your table I'd heard him on his phone—'

Lycos slapped his hand down on the table. Cutting her off. 'Arielle. Enough. I am not going to repeat myself. He could have cut his losses at any time and folded. He didn't. It was his choice, his responsibility, his problem.'

He took a scything breath.

'I'm not discussing it any more. If I gamble again, I won't take you with me since it obviously upsets you so much.'

He took another breath, less scything this time.

'Now, let's just relax, OK?'

He reached for the wine, topped up their glasses and drank from his own. He glanced across at Arielle again. She'd gone quiet, and he should be glad of it, but relaxed she was not. He wanted her relaxed.

'So,' he opened, deliberately moving on and away from what had so unnecessarily upset her. 'What would you like to do tomorrow? Shall we even stay in Paris? If you've seen enough, we could head out to Normandy, Brittany, down to the Loire? What appeals? You choose,' he said invitingly.

'I don't know,' she said.

'Or maybe we could head east, tour the Champagne vineyards if you prefer,' he suggested.

'I... I don't know.'

'Well, we can decide tomorrow. Right now, that tiramisu is calling!' he said good-humouredly.

He cleared their plates, spooned out generous portions of the tiramisu and poured out the dessert wine to go with it. He tucked into both heartily. Arielle less so. As she pushed her plate aside, he reached across, drew the back of his fingers softly down her cheek. Hunger was flaring in him again for Arielle.

She drew back. Looked across at him, but with that shuttered, half look again.

'Lycos, I... I'm sorry. I'm going to have to take some aspirin. My head just isn't clearing. I'm sorry,' she said again.

Lycos breathed out, subduing his own feelings. 'No need to apologise. Do you have any? Any aspirin, or anything else?'

She stood up. 'Yes, in my toilet bag. I won't be a moment.' She disappeared into the bathroom. Lycos remained sitting at the table. This wasn't about a headache. This was about the evening that had passed. This was about the Wolf.

But it's who I am. And if she didn't like it...?

Impatiently, he brushed the question away. It didn't need to be answered.

It's got nothing to do with what there is between us.

Nor would he let it be.

CHAPTER ELEVEN

ARIELLE STOOD BY the river's edge, leaning on the stone wall between her and the water. She'd slept heavily, thanks to the aspirin she'd taken, but sleep had not refreshed her. She'd awoken, Lycos asleep still, and despite the early hour she'd crept from the bed. She'd pulled on some random clothes, then slipped from the room and walked out of the hotel. She'd wanted to be on her own with her troubling thoughts.

She watched the river flow past her, heading to the sea. There was the slightest chill in this early morning air, reminding the city that autumn was on the way. A sudden, painful memory assailed her. At the *mas*, at this hour, she'd be stirring, preparing to get up and head out to let out the poultry and collect any eggs.

Lycos loved those omelettes with the eggs so fresh...

The image was vivid in her mind's eye. Sitting outside, under the faded awning, Lycos tucking into his omelette before moving on to croissants with home-made apricot jam and butter from Jeanne and Claude's cows.

She felt her heart squeeze painfully. How happy she had been then. Day after day after day. Night after night after night. One week eliding into the next and the next and the next. An endless time, it had seemed.

I will remember it all my life. Never again will I know such happiness.

Because never again would she be able to call the *Mas Delfine* her home.

Or have Lycos in her life.

Regret filled her. She should have found the courage to talk to Lycos, to ask him to his face what she meant to him. Whether she meant anything at all other than a passing romance. Beguiled by the peaceful beauty of the *mas*. Indulging her here in this lavish stay in Paris.

But did that matter any longer?

The very question was hard to face. Last night she had seen a side of him she had known about, but hadn't realised just what it meant. Now she did.

I've seen the Wolf. Seen what he does.

Her brow furrowed as she stared down at the turbid waters of the river. Emotions, as turbid as the river, made their presence felt. Heavy and hard to face.

But face them she must.

Slowly, she turned away, returning to the hotel. To Lycos. To say to him what she must.

Lycos stirred, his hand automatically going across the bed to reach Arielle. He had been consideration itself last night, letting her sleep peacefully, curled up on the far side of the bed. It hadn't been the way he'd wanted to spend the night, but he wouldn't have dreamt of pestering her.

Nor would he now, either. Instead, he'd enquire sympathetically how she was feeling and whether she was up to breakfast. Up to doing anything that day.

But as his hand reached across, he realised she wasn't in the bed at all. He sat up, looking around. She wasn't visible. The bathroom door was open and clearly empty. He frowned and reached for his phone. He sent her a quick text.

Are you OK?

It took a moment for a reply to come through.

Fine. I just wanted some fresh air. I'm heading back now.

Relieved, he replied with a simple text.

Great. Are you up for breakfast?

Again, the reply took a moment.

Fine, thanks.

He sent back a thumbs up emoji and rang down for breakfast to be brought up, as it was every day.

They had breakfast at leisure, in bed, and took their time over it. And sometimes took yet more time to get the day underway. Making love to Arielle in the morning light was memorable indeed.

No, best not think of that. She might still have a headache.

Instead, he used the time to take a quick shower and

shave, and throw on a fresh tee shirt and boxers. As breakfast arrived, so did Arielle. He smiled encouragingly at her and the moment they were alone he immediately asked how she was feeling.

'I'm OK,' she said.

But she didn't look OK. She looked the way she had last night. Withdrawn, not making eye contact.

Different.

He looked at her. 'Arielle, what is it? You're upset. And don't say it's just a headache. It's more than that.'

She went to the window and looked out for a moment. Her shoulders seemed hunched. She turned back to him.

'I think it's time I left for England,' she said.

She had said it. Said what had been building up in her ever since she'd woken, unable to get back to sleep, hearing Lycos's steady breathing beside her. So near to her and yet so far.

He was staring at her now. His face had shuttered. It reminded her of how he'd looked last night.

'Why?' he asked bluntly.

She bit her lip. 'I just think it's the right time,' she said.

'Why?' he asked again.

She swallowed.

'Because—'

She stopped, twisted her hands and met his eyes, though it was hard to do. She took a breath, a difficult one.

'Lycos, this time with you has been...amazing. Fantastic. Wonderful. Unforgettable. But...'

She paused again, then made herself say it.

'It was never going to last, was it? It was always a kind

of, well, accident really. You just turned up at the *mas* on impulse. A place you'd never chosen to own. A place that just landed on you. Then you saw me there, and I was… well, as attracted to you as you were to me. So, we, well… We started an affair.'

She drew a deep breath and looked him in the eye. 'But I never had any…expectations because of it. Because…' She broke off again.

She gave a smile, a wry one, that hid far more than she was prepared to let him see.

'Lycos, you're not just the Wolf. You're the Lone Wolf.'

She took another breath. 'And I know that. I know that our time at the *mas* was just a holiday to you. Just as showing me Paris was. It was a time out from the life you lead. That life like the race day, like that party last night. You cruise around, enjoying your wealth and why not? You've made it by your own efforts, you deserve to enjoy it! And in my time with you I've enjoyed it too. This lovely hotel, all those expensive restaurants and wearing the expensive clothes you bought me. I won't pretend otherwise. But nor will I pretend that I mean anything more to you than any of my…predecessors. That's why you're a Lone Wolf.'

She continued to look directly at him before finishing, 'And that's why it's time for me to head to England. I have to make a new life for myself. You told me that and you're right. The *mas* has gone. It will never be in my life again. It will never be mine.'

Lycos was looking at her, meeting her gaze full on. She could not read his expression. She was too focussed on saying what she was saying, making herself say it, knowing she had to say it. As she fell silent, he finally got to his feet and moved over to her. He stood right in front of her and took her hands in his.

'What if it were?' he said.

Her first reaction was no reaction, her expression entirely blank. He repeated what he'd just said.

'What if it were? What if the *mas* was yours?'

He kept his voice neutral, entirely neutral. Deadpan, like his expression.

But deadpan was not what he was feeling. When she'd made that announcement, *I think it's time I left for England*, it was like a punch landing in his solar plexus. It came out of nowhere and winded him so he could not breathe.

But he'd forced himself to breathe. Forced himself to reply. To challenge her. Demolish what she'd just said by any means necessary.

And what he'd just said now was necessary.

In cards, in gaming, sometimes you had to set the stakes high. Higher than you intended, or preferred, in order to net your opponent and to keep them in the game. All so that you could win in the end.

And winning, now, was essential.

Because if I lose—

No, he could not think like that. Did not dare to. Too much was at stake.

Not the *mas*. Something far more crucial. Vital to him.

Something that, until this moment, he had not realised just how vital it was to him.

Arielle.

He heard her name echo in his head. Felt emotion knife

through him, like a dagger thrust, but he pulled the blade from himself. He had to focus only on what he had to achieve. By any means necessary. By staking what he was now prepared to stake. By reminding himself about who he was.

I am the Wolf. And I do not lose.

He watched her face and saw the frown form above her eyes.

'I don't understand,' she said.

'It's very simple,' he said. His voice was calm. Very calm. The way he was at the gaming table. Preternaturally calm. 'I don't want you to go.'

She looked at him. He still could not read her expression. But he could feel her hands in his. They felt cold. Inert.

'Why?' His earlier question to her echoed back to him.

'Because we're good together. And I want that to continue.' He pressed her hands, still cold, still inert. His eyes locked on to hers, willing her to accept what he was saying. 'Arielle, I don't want you to leave me. I want you to stay with me. I want you to want to stay with me. So, I want you to have something you want.' He took a breath, looked right at her. He wanted to make it clear to her what he was prepared to stake. 'If I give you the *mas*, give you back your home, the home that was taken from you, will you stay with me?'

She stilled completely.

Then he felt her slip her hands from his. Step back.

And what was in her face he could not understand.

Nor bear to see—

Arielle sat, her eyes closed, as the Eurostar sped towards Calais, and she could only urge it on desperately.

Lest she detrain at Lille and head right back to Paris. To Lycos.

Her throat closed. Tension wracked through her, along with misery and unhappiness.

And so, so much longing. Longing to undo what she had said to Lycos. To unsay the words. The words she had delivered like the stab from a knife. She heard them again now, all of them. Each one cruel and heartless. And true.

But there was no taking them back. Just as there was no way to deny the implication of what he had said to her.

Or the price she would pay for it.

He would be buying me.

Because what else would it be? He was offering her the one thing in the world she wanted so, so much.

But to accept it for such a reason? To accept it at all—

She heard her own voice, recoiling.

'You can't mean that. You cannot possibly mean that. How can you even think it?'

He'd sounded bewildered as he'd riposted.

'But it's what you want. You've said it a hundred times!'

And then her own voice vehement in protest.

'Of course I can't accept it! And for such a reason—'

Now, as her words replayed in her head, she knew, with a flush of shame, that she should have said more.

That I had given him every reason to think he could make an offer like that to me. Why shouldn't he think that? He swept me up into his luxury lifestyle. Wined and dined me at expensive restaurants and picked up the tab for ev-

erything. Paid for all those couture clothes he bought for me to wear, that diamond pendant and all the jewellery he said he wanted to buy for me.

Buy me with—

Her face contorted. Oh, she had told herself she was only letting him make her look so expensively glamorous to show how far he'd come from being that abused, neglected, impoverished boy from the backstreets of Athens, but she'd worn them all the same, hadn't she? She'd let him lavish his wealth on her and she'd gone along with all of it. No wonder he'd thought he could offer to give her the *mas*.

Buy her with that.

Anguish stabbed her, piercing through the flush of shame. Filling her with a longing so great, a sense of loss so deep, that she could not bear it.

I could have had Lycos. And my home back.

Her nails dug into the palms of her hands and she welcomed the pain. Deserved it.

Because he offered me exactly what I had dreamt of! That stupid, dangerous dream that he and I could make our home at the mas. *That I would lose neither him, nor my home.*

Yet the offer he'd made her had been poison.

Her cruel denunciation of him rang in her ears.

'You've tried to buy me, Lycos! And I'm appalled by it! I've never thought you capable of that! Just like I never thought you capable of behaving the way you did last night, demolishing that wretched boy! You should have refused to play with him! You're hard and callous and

ruthless and I've seen a side of you I don't like, and I don't want to be with!'

He'd made no reply, no defence. Only watched her, his face closed, as she'd snatched up her clothes—her own clothes, not the couture outfits that his money had purchased—stuffing them into her suitcase. At the door she'd turned. He hadn't moved. Her eyes had rested on him, stony and implacable, as she'd told him, *'I'm sorry. Sorry it's come to this. Sorry it's ended like this. Just...sorry.'*

She'd been unable to say more and what more had there been to say? Except one last thing. Her voice broken.

'I didn't know you, Lycos. I thought I did, but I didn't. Now I do.'

She'd walked out and he'd made no attempt to stop her.

And that, she knew as she felt tears sting like acid beneath her tightly closed eyelids and as the Eurostar bore her relentlessly away from him, had been the worst of all...

CHAPTER TWELVE

LYCOS NOSED HIS car forward along the stony driveway. It had rained recently and the sky was overcast. Getting out of the car he felt the chill of the mistral on his back—the cold north-westerly wind that plagued Provence in the autumn and winter. He looked about him.

The *mas* looked drear and deserted. The faded blue shutters were closed on all the windows and the stone walls un-warmed by any sunshine.

He felt the hollow inside him gape wider.

It had been there for a long, long time now. It had started as he'd watched Arielle walking out of the hotel bedroom, not believing that she was doing so. The shock of it knifing through him, hollowing him out.

He hadn't known what to do.

Nor did he still.

He stood staring at the *mas*, trying to work out what he felt, but it was impossible. The hollow inside him seemed to make him numb. He went into the courtyard, the cobbles wet from rain, his footsteps ringing damply on the stone.

It was very quiet and deserted. The livestock was all gone, having been transported to the neighbouring farm.

He walked through into the gardens. The rain and autumn had bleached the colour from it. The lavender was full of brown deadheads. The geraniums were limp and drooping. The leaves from the trees remained un-swept and unraked. The pool had been covered over, the sun loungers packed away. Water dripped off the roses, which were bereft of any blooms.

He stood awhile, the hollow widening within him.

Becoming wide enough to swallow him up completely.

What am I to do?

The words took physical shape in his head. Hanging there as if heavy weights.

He had come here for one purpose only. To put the place behind him. To put it on the market as he had always said he would do.

To get rid of it.

It was the logical thing to do. It always had been. He hadn't asked for this place, hadn't sought it out, hadn't chosen it. It had just happened to him. Owning it as he did.

So, getting rid of it, taking the money, was the obvious thing to do.

So why haven't I?

The logic, now, was even more compelling, ineluctable, necessary. After all, his conscience was clear. Completely clear.

I offered it to her and she turned it down.

Turned down not just the mas, *but turned me down with it.*

He felt the hollow gape wider yet, but something was filling it now. Something worse than the hollow. The hollow was an absence, but this... This was a presence. An unbearable one. An agonising one.

And suddenly, with a clenching of his fists buried in the pockets of his jacket that was keeping at bay the chill of the mistral, he knew what he would do. Must do.

After all, had he not already done elsewhere what he must do? This would complete it.

For one lone, last moment he let his gaze rest on the garden in front of him before looking around and across the frontage of the *mas*. Then, with rapid and resolute footsteps, he headed back to his car and drove away.

He was done with the *mas*.

For the *mas* was done with him. Just like Arielle was.

Arielle opened her voicemail. The call had come in while she'd been expounding French irregular verbs to the adult education class she taught, which, together with the modest income from her father that had funded her at the *mas*, was funding her there in England. It was strange to be back in the university town where she'd studied music, but it was the only place in England that she was familiar with. Other than London, where her father had lived and worked, and London was way out of her price range. Here she could afford to rent a small flat and pay for the use of a nearby church hall, which came with a piano, so she could give piano lessons. She had also applied to start training to be a teacher so she'd be able to teach French and music at the local school.

It was not the life she'd wanted, but she knew she had to make it work. Perhaps, one day, she'd be inspired to do something more. But in that moment, she was still too raw. Far, far too raw.

Raw with loss. A loss that the passing weeks had shown her was far, far worse than she had once thought it would be.

Because what I had, is gone and will never, can never, return. And what I had was far, far more than I realised I had.

She felt her heart clench, pain filling it. With a heavy sigh she held the phone to her ear. She frowned. The voicemail was from her lawyer, the one she'd spent money she could not afford on when she'd contested her father's will. What could the matter be now? Surely Naomi wasn't trying, again, to get hold of the money her husband had dared to bestow on his daughter, not herself?

But the message was quite different. And when she heard it Arielle could only stare, blankly and disbelievingly. But with something flaring inside her that had not been there before.

Lycos sat in the cocktail lounge of the hotel on Park Lane. It was where he usually stayed when he was in London, for it boasted a casino on the top floor. This time he hadn't been near it. It held no attraction for him. His mind was focussed on one thing only.

Would she come?

Tension wracked him. It reminded him of his early days, setting out to make his way in the world with his card skills before he had learnt to step aside from all emotion. Before he'd learnt how to move into the mental state that detached him from the world and generated the intense focus of concentration necessary to his purpose.

But detachment, now, was impossible. Too much was at stake. More than he had ever thought would be or could be. Because that was what this was, he knew, with a scything inbreath. A stake higher than he had ever made in all his life. Memories bit in him, like the bite of a wolf. Back in Paris, all those weeks ago, he'd made a stake he'd thought must surely be irresistible.

But it lost me what I most wanted.

What he had most wanted then.

But now?

His thoughts cut out. His gaze fixed on the entrance to the cocktail lounge.

Arielle got off the bus. Autumnal chill hit her at once, raw and unpleasant. A world away from the summer's heat of Provence. She could feel emotion churn inside her as she walked into the hotel. A sudden, vivid memory of the Viscari Paris assailed her—the evening she and Lycos had dined with the Derenzes.

She looked around the lobby, wondering where the cocktail bar was. Then she saw it and made her way to it. She stepped inside, aware that her heart was thudding like hammers in her chest.

Lycos got to his feet. Arielle was heading towards him. He felt something catch within him, across the hollow that was permanently there. Just to see her again. His gaze clung to her as she approached. But he would not let it show in his eyes.

'Thank you for coming,' he said, as she reached him. He kept his voice carefully neutral.

She gave only a slight nod, sitting down in the tub chair opposite his. The light level in the cocktail bar was subdued, but he could see she looked pale. The honeyed skin tone he was familiar with had faded, it seemed, out of the Provençal sun. Her hair was drawn back into a pleat and was glistening with faint raindrops. She slipped the buttons of her jacket undone, but did not remove it. Yet even looking as workaday as she was, he still felt his breath catch at seeing her again. Seeing her beauty...

But he must not show his reaction to her. That was not why he had asked her to meet him. A waiter glided up, asking what she would like to drink. She asked for coffee then looked across the low table. Straight at him.

'Why did you do it, Lycos? This time?'

The question was direct. So was his answer.

'Because it was the right thing to do. Because it was owed to you.'

She gave a shake of her head. 'Not by you. You owe me nothing, Lycos.' She took a heavy, scything breath before continuing, 'Least of all *Mas Delfine*.'

Arielle did not let her eyes drop. Would not. She had been here before with this conversation. And, although the reason for it had been completely different, her answer was the same.

'You know that I can't accept it, Lycos,' she said, her voice low. 'Any more than the last time you offered it to me.'

'Now is completely different! You must see that!' he

cut across her. His voice was vehement and his eyes flared with anger.

'Your motive is different, yes, but it's still one I can't accept.'

She held his gaze. It was hard to do so. Hard to sit here, so close to him, seeing him again, suppressing all that she felt about him. Those feelings had flared again the moment she'd seen him as she'd walked into the cocktail lounge. Flared as powerfully as they ever had. As they always would—

Because they will. I know that now. It doesn't matter that I ended it before he was ready to end it. It doesn't matter that I have not seen him for weeks and weeks. That I am making myself make a new life here in England— the one I have to make. That the memory of our time together will haunt me all my days and my longing for him will haunt me all my nights.

Just seeing him again, here and now, was hammering home that truth. Just as her heart was hammering in her chest.

Just to see him. Just to be here with him.

Emotion crushed her heart, fight it though she must. She had come here because he had asked her to and to refuse would have been ungracious.

Cowardly. Thinking more of her own feelings, than on the gesture he had just made to her. She ploughed on, saying what she knew had to be said. What she knew she had to make clear to him. She kept her voice as calm as she could.

'Lycos, I can only repeat what you yourself said to me. That it is not your fault that you own the *mas*. My mother sold it to my father, he left it to Naomi, she gave it to Gerald. You won it off him because he was an arrogant fool to play you. So, he deserved to lose.'

Lycos was looking at her. 'That's not how you felt about that boy in Paris.'

She frowned. Why had he said that now?

'Well, he was a fool, too, but a terrified one. He was desperate.'

'And now I know why.'

Arielle stared. 'What do you mean?'

Lycos leant forward, picked up his martini glass, took a mouthful. Then replaced it. He seemed hesitant to speak at first but then he did.

'After you'd gone, I went to see him,' he said.

Her eyes widened. 'You did what?'

'I went to see him. I got the hotel concierge to find me his Paris address, a very upmarket apartment in the 7th *arrondissement*, and I called on him.' He paused again, then continued. 'When he opened the door to me, he went white at the gills. But he invited me in, took control of himself, went and got a chequebook from a desk and told me he would write me a cheque for the sum of the IOU. He assumed that's why I'd turned up.'

'Had you?'

'No. I took his IOU out of my jacket pocket and tore it up. Then I handed him a banker's draft for the value of the chips he'd lost to me and told him that if he was smart, he'd lay off gambling, or he'd be an even bigger fool than he'd been that night.'

Arielle could only stare. 'What...what did he say?'

'He didn't. Not then. Someone came into the room. A

teenage girl, looking just as scared as he did. He said she was his sister. He told her I'd torn up his IOU and given him back the money he'd lost.' He paused again. Arielle could hear the change in his voice. 'She burst into tears.'

He took a breath. He was looking right at Arielle.

'It all came out. She said their mother had been scammed out of a huge amount of money and if their father found out he'd be furious. He was a bully and made their mother's life hell. So, the boy was desperate to cover his mother's losses. Desperate enough to scrape together all the money he could, without their father finding out, and try his luck at the tables. But they'd only made things worse. He lost everything they'd scraped together to bet with that evening.'

He reached for his martini and took another slug before looking across at Arielle again.

'I've ended up giving him a loan. That, along with the sum he'd gambled away, should cover their mother's losses.'

Arielle stared. 'You did that for someone you don't even know?'

He put down his martini glass. Gave a half shrug. 'I'd thought him a cocky, arrogant, aristocratic idiot who was showing off by taking me on at cards.' He paused. 'I was wrong.'

He reached inside his jacket pocket, took out an envelope and opened it. He removed a piece of paper from it and something else.

'He gave me his IOU for the loan I made him. He'll make me regular payments out of his allowance, he's still a student, and for anything still outstanding his trust fund matures when he's twenty-five. But he also gave me this as surety. It's his pledge of honour.'

He held out to Arielle the gold, crested signet ring she'd seen the boy wearing. She touched it briefly, wonderingly, and Lycos put it away again in the envelope with the IOU. Thoughts tumbled through her head. More than thoughts. Words came to her. Words she'd said to him as she'd leant her head on his shoulder that night at the *mas* after they'd pitched in with the grape harvest and Lycos had said he'd promised Dan a spin in his flash car.

'*You're a good man, Lycos Dimistrios,*' she'd said.

She said it again now, her voice low. Her eyes holding his.

He gave a faint smile. 'I'm trying to be,' he said. 'Your words stung. That's why I went to see him.' His voice changed again as he continued. 'And it's why I want to restore your home to you.'

He drew a breath.

'This time, Arielle, I'm not trying to buy you.'

Her face constricted.

'I let you think I could be bought,' she said, her voice low. 'I let you lavish your money on me. Buy me beautiful clothes and jewellery. I told myself I was doing it just to please you. That it didn't matter and didn't mean anything. But when you offered me the *mas* so I would stay with you. Oh, Lycos...' her voice broke. 'You were offering me the one thing I longed for. The one thing in the world I wanted most except for...'

She broke off. Suddenly realising what she'd been about to blurt out.

The arrival of her coffee saved her. She dropped her

eyes and busied herself stirring in the sachet of sugar, giving herself precious moments to recover and to feel she could look at Lycos again.

His gaze was still on her, but there was something different about him. Something that made her think of his nickname, as if he were a wolf indeed that had just picked up an unexpected scent. A scent he had not known existed...

But which he would not now relinquish.

'Except for what?'

His words fell into the silence. His eyes held hers. Held her helpless. Defeated. Her expression changed. She set down her coffee spoon.

'Except for you, Lycos,' she said.

He heard her speak. Heard the words. But they made no sense.

'Why do you say that?' he said. A frown creased his brow. His breath was frozen in his lungs, but he spoke again. 'It was you who left me,' he said. 'Even before I offered you your home back.'

She broke eye contact, her gaze slipping away across the room.

'Lycos, right from the start I told myself our affair would be just that. An affair, nothing more. That it would end and then, just as you'd told me I must, I would have to go to England and make a new life for myself. Even if you did spend some more time with me in Normandy, or wherever, the end would still be the same. So—'

He saw her pick up her coffee spoon and put it down again. She looked across at him again.

'So when I got upset, after that horrible gaming party, I felt I couldn't stay with you any longer.'

Something changed in her face. Something that it hurt him to see.

'Then...when you'd offered me the *mas* to stay with you I knew my decision was the only one I could make.'

Her voice dropped, twisting, 'I could never stay with a man who thought I could be bought.'

He was silent. The gaping hollow that had been inside him ever since he'd watched her walk out of his hotel room, out of his life, stretched like a chasm that must swallow him. He could not bridge it, yet he must try. However hard it was to find the words.

'Arielle...' he said her name tentatively, unsurely, '...I made you that offer...because...because I panicked.'

She stared at him, incomprehension in her face.

'You were going to leave me,' he said. 'And I panicked.' His face worked. 'Arielle, you said you never thought there was anything between us but an affair. If I'd put anything into words, even to myself, I would probably have thought the same. We were good together, that's what I thought. That's what I said to you. You were like no other woman I'd known. You were not like the women such as Natalie, who hang around wealthy men. I didn't really think much more beyond that. Until...'

He took another breath. 'Until you said you were leaving. Until I realised I had lost you. And that it was my own fault.'

He looked away for a moment, out over the cocktail lounge. Then his eyes came back to her. Nothing had changed in her face. Nothing at all. He felt the gaping hollow inside him still.

'I went back to the *mas*, determined to put it up for sale because I could not bear the memories there tormenting me.'

His expression changed.

'But then, I realised that there was only one thing to be done with the *mas*. To make amends.'

He reached inside his jacket pocket, drew out a thick envelope and took out the document within.

'It's the title deeds to *Mas Delfine*,' he said. 'All authorised by the *notaire* and made out in your name.'

She shook her head. 'I can't, Lycos. I can't.' It was a whisper, nothing more, and in her eyes was a look of anguish. 'There are no amends to make. I understand, now, why you made that offer to me in Paris.'

Slowly, very slowly, he felt for the words he needed now. The words he needed to close that gaping hollow inside him and seal it for ever.

'Do you, Arielle? Do you understand why I was desperate for you not to leave me?'

He swallowed. Painful, as if he were swallowing glass.

'In Paris, you called me the Lone Wolf. And I have been, Arielle, all my life. You know my origins, that neither parent cared about me. That because I knew I was unimportant, was not valued by them, I made my way in the world not caring about anyone else. Oh, I hope I was never…callous towards any of the women I consorted with, women like Natalie. I dealt with them on their own terms and it was enough, so it seemed.'

He paused again. Fixed his eyes on her. Her face

was very pale and her expression unreadable. He took a breath. He knew what he must say. And that if he said it he may risk it all. But he knew he had to make his final stake.

'But with you, Arielle, it was not enough. I wanted more. So much more.'

He felt his throat tighten and he had to force the words past. These were the most important words he was ever going to say in his life.

'After all our time together, those timeless days at the *mas* and then in Paris, I wanted never to be the Lone Wolf again.'

Her expression hadn't changed, but her face had whitened, like chalk.

He continued, 'That was why I was so desperate you should not leave me.'

He dropped his gaze to the thickly folded paper on the table, the deeds to *Mas Delfine*. He had to find more words. Slowly, feeling his heart thudding inside him, he pushed the deeds towards her. Lifted his eyes to her again.

His eyes, he knew, showed all the emotions that he felt. All that was in him and always would be. All that he felt for her.

He swallowed, finding the words that meant everything to him and always would.

'What if the *mas* were my wedding present to you?'

Arielle heard him say it. How could she not? Yet there seemed to be something wrong with her hearing. There was a drumming in her head, in her ears, drowning out everything.

'A...a wedding present?' She said it as if no such thing could ever exist.

Her eyes were locked on his and in his gaze she saw something that made her weak. He lifted his hand, as if to reach to her. His voice was low and urgent.

'Arielle, you told me that I was the only thing you wanted more than *Mas Delfine*. I feel the same about you.' He took a ragged breath before continuing. 'Except that, there is nothing else, absolutely nothing else, that can possibly compete with me wanting you.' He took a breath, another ragged one. 'Loving you.'

His eyes bored into hers. 'Because that is what it is. What I now know it to be. I couldn't see it at the time. I needed the hell I've been in since you left me in Paris to show me that! To show me that wanting you, loving you, is all I could ever want. For all my life. Wanting you as the heart of my heart, the love of my life, as my wife. If you will have me?'

Tears, slow and misting, were welling in her eyes and spilling down her cheeks. He reached forwards with his hand and brushed them away with the tips of his fingers.

'Is that a yes?' he asked, his voice quizzical.

How could he ask? How could he even *ask*? Her tears flowed faster and she heard him mutter an oath. Saw him, through her now hopelessly blurred vision, get to his feet, hunker down beside her and catch her hand, holding it fast. She squeezed it tight, as if she would never let it go, for she never would now. She cried for quite a while. He remained hunkered down beside her, saying nothing, just holding her hand as tightly as she was holding his. So much was going through her mind. So, so much.

She had never dared to admit it, to face that she had fallen in love with him, that to have lost him as she had was unbearable. But now, Lycos was hers. Hers for ever. And she was his for ever.

And the *mas*, her beloved *Mas Delfine*, was no longer his, but nor was it hers, either. Because it was going to be what would bring her more joy than anything in the world, except for Lycos. Except for loving Lycos and being loved by Lycos.

It will be ours.

Theirs for ever. As they were to each other.

Her tears were drying and her heart was singing— singing and soaring. She had gone there that evening to tell Lycos she had no claim on the *mas*. That she could not accept his offer, whatever the reasons he gave and however generous he wanted to be.

She had gone with the expectation that seeing him again would be agony and the knowledge that she had to walk away again from him.

But now, I never shall. Never!

Lycos drew her to her feet. Helplessly, she let him. The world was still a blur, her body suddenly weak. He let slip her hand, but only to slide his arm around her waist and draw her against his side.

'I've got a room here, *Mme* Dimistrios-to-be,' he informed her. In his voice was the husk she was so familiar with. She looked up at him, into his night-dark eyes.

He brushed her lips lightly, so lightly with his that her body trembled with it.

'So, though the hour is early, shall we retire?'

She gave a sigh of bliss, of happiness, of wonder and of love.

'Oh, yes,' she breathed. 'Oh, yes.'

Her body was silk and satin, her mouth velvet and her caresses like a living flame to rouse him to all that he longed for. With his lips and the tips of his fingers, he paid homage to her. From the tender lobes of her ears, down the slender column of her throat, to the sweet mounds of her breasts with their coral peaks straining at his touch and down the valley between. Down, down, to the deeper valley as her thighs slackened and he sought, and found, all that gave delight. To her. To him.

And as their bodies fused and flamed, and as they both cried out, he knew with every fibre of his body, every beat of his hectic heart, every breath and every blaze of all that filled him, that here was his heart's desire. His heart's fulfilment.

She lay in his arms, the woman he knew he loved, could never live without and now never needed to. Her tears were wet again on his naked torso and he cradled her to him. As close as they could be. As if they were one body, with a single beating heart.

'Is this love?' she whispered. 'Is this really, really love?'

He grazed her lips with his.

'Oh, yes,' he said with a smile on his lips and in his voice, and a look of love in his eyes. 'Oh, yes.'

She gave a sigh of heart's content. And so did he.

And sleep, the sleep of love's sweet promise, took them both.

EPILOGUE

The following summer...

'OH, MAURICE, THERE IS no need to look like that at me! Your little ones are safe here! Mathilde can teach them to swim in the swimming pool! You know I won't say no!'

Arielle's voice was a mix of resignation and amusement.

Beside her, Lycos laughed. 'They've timed their brood well. I'm sure Marc and Tara's children will be enchanted to share the pool with ducklings!'

They both watched awhile as Mathilde shepherded her precious offspring bobbing about adorably in the azure water and Maurice marched protectively, and self-importantly, along the edge of the pool.

Arielle and Lycos left them to it. The Derenzes would be arriving the next day, en route to their villa on Cap Saint-Pierre, where Arielle and Lycos were invited to join them later in the month. The couple had become friends and Arielle was glad of it, for her own sake. She'd hit it off with the plain-speaking Tara from the start. And for Lycos's sake too because it drew him away from those he knew from the casino circuit.

Although those on the casino circuit were not all as repellent as she'd originally thought, she had to allow as she'd come to know them better. Some were merely wealthy and enjoyed exercising skill at cards, either casually or, like Lycos himself, more seriously.

Not that Lycos gambled seriously any longer. Now he only did it, as he had told her, to keep his skill up and for the satisfaction of pitting his wits against worthy opponents. But he was choosy about with whom he gambled—only those he was certain could afford to lose to him.

Arielle's expression changed as they made their way across the terrace. She and Lycos had made another couple of friends since their rapturous reunion last autumn. Young Gervais de Lascaux, over whom Lycos was keeping an eye as he steadily repaid his loan, and his sister, Marie-Claire, had remained in touch. They had met up socially in Paris, along with their mother, the *vicomtesse*, whose tearful gratitude to Lycos had touched Arielle. As had her children's devotion to her. They, too, would be making a visit to *Mas Delfine* later in the year.

Mas Delfine. Arielle's expression softened as it always did when she thought of her beloved home. *Their* beloved home. Hers and Lycos's. Lycos. Her husband. Her *beloved* husband. No longer, and never again, what she had once sadly called him—the Lone Wolf.

No, he was not that man any more. He had found his mate, his companion for life. As had she.

Wonder and happiness filled her.

They had married without delay. A small, private ceremony uniting them legally, just as their own hearts had already united them emotionally. They had honeymooned in Normandy, the lush countryside resplendent in autumnal glory. And Lycos had taken her to see what he'd told her was her second wedding present. Her eyes had widened as they'd arrived.

'I've bought land for paddocks and built stabling,' he'd told her. 'And hired staff to run it. It's a rescue and rehab centre for retired and discarded racehorses.' He'd paused. 'Come and meet the first resident.'

He'd led the way forward to a spacious loosebox where a handsome gelding whinnied in greeting.

'I bought him from Paul Ronsard before he'd had time to have him put down. Paul thought me a fool.' Lycos shrugged indifferently. He no longer socialised with Paul and did not miss him.

Arielle lifted her hand to the velvet muzzle. 'Hello, boy,' she said softly. 'Now you can run only for pleasure, not profit.' She turned to Lycos, her face expressive. 'You are a good, good man, Lycos Dimistrios,' she said. Her eyes were alight with love.

Lycos patted the steed's neck. 'Those we take in who can be repurposed, so to speak, for hacking can be passed on to careful owners. But the others can simply live out their lives here in comfort and safety.'

'It must be costing you a fortune!' Arielle said, concern in her voice.

Lycos shrugged again. 'Now, when I gamble, all my winnings go here,' he said.

She kissed his cheek. 'Then I hope the Wolf never loses!' she told him.

He cupped her face with his hands, eyes boring into

hers. 'I have won the most precious treasure of all,' he said. 'Your heart.'

She raised her mouth to his, brushing lightly. 'And yours is mine,' she said. 'And always will be.'

Love swelled within her, as it always did, as she slipped her hand into his.

They walked together through the archway into the cobbled yard beyond. The hens were pecking about on the rough ground beyond the gateway where Lycos's monster car was parked up. It had been well exercised earlier in the week, for it had been Jeanne and Claude's petrolhead teenage son Dan's birthday and Lycos had treated him to a thrilling track day so he could experience driving it himself. Though insured to the eyeballs, Jeanne had confided to Arielle that she was grateful Dan could never aspire to own such an expensive, and so dangerously powerful, car.

In exchange for the track day for his son, Claude was teaching Lycos to drive a different vehicle—a tractor. Lycos was buying one of his own. A top of the range vehicle to go with the ATV he'd purchased in the spring. Both were to come into use as Lycos busied himself with his next preoccupation. He was going to develop a *vin Delfine* from newly-planted vineyards on land he'd bought from neighbours, on the far side of the *mas* away from Jeanne and Claude, which had also once been part of Arielle's family property long ago.

Lycos was not just buying back former land and involving himself in the local wine-growers association, he was also restoring the barns in the courtyard—despite the objections from drake Maurice and cockerel Jean-Paul at the disruption.

At the same time, Arielle was carefully, but assiduously, updating the *mas* itself. It was a complete labour of love and she was taking great care to make sure that the restoration was an *homage* and not a modernisation. The plumbing had been updated, the electrics and appliances converted to solar power supplied by out-of-view panels, but the *décor*, even when repainted and worn fabrics replaced, retained its old-world charm. Her piano, too, retained its place of honour in the parlour. Lycos had donated a fine instrument in its place to the *lycée*, where Arielle gave piano lessons *gratis* to those not able to afford them otherwise. Here, though, she still loved to while away an evening at her own piano, her father's gift to her, soothing Lycos with Schumann and Chopin.

Until, as always happened, she would see a glint form in his night-dark eyes and know that something more than music was drawing his attention. Then she would close down the lid, move gracefully towards him as he got to his feet, taking her hands. The glint in his eye telling her there was only one destination for them both then… Until the morning light brought a new day.

Day, after day, after day. An endless succession now, for all the rest of their lives. Gratitude and love poured through her at how happy, how blissfully happy, they were. Every day she gave thanks that Lycos the Wolf had played that fateful game of cards with her stepbrother and had won *Mas Delfine*.

Or he would never have come into my life. The mas *would have been sold and I would have lost it for ever.*

And if Gerald hadn't sold it, the *mas* might have been seized as an asset. She gave a shiver. Not long after they'd got married Lycos told her that Naomi's fourth husband, yet another wealthy businessman whom she had married shortly after the funeral of Arielle's father, had been arrested on charges of fraud and corruption. Naomi, and Gerald, had flagrantly invested Charles Frobisher's legacy into the latest husband's business. As a result, not only had all their assets been frozen, but both Naomi and Gerald had been implicated in the malfeasance and would stand trial. Prison sentences for both loomed.

Arielle tried not to be glad, but Lycos was blunt.

'Nemesis,' he said roundly. 'The Greek goddess of retribution. They had it coming.'

Arielle let it be. Thanks to Lycos the *mas* was safe. And, thanks to Lycos and the love they shared, she would be happy now and all her life. And so would he. And for yet one more reason—

She felt her heart lift as they went into the kitchen. The dresser still held pride of place, freshly repainted, but the ancient range had been replaced by one that would see out another generation at least. The new, low-energy fridge no longer grumbled to itself. The water gushing from the new, but old-styled brass taps over the new, but still stone sink, still came from the ancient well, but it was pumped up now using solar power.

Companionably, she and Lycos assembled their salad lunch with leaves freshly picked, tomatoes and peaches likewise and cheeses, as always, from Jeanne's dairy. As they did every day when the weather was clement, they took lunch out to the shaded ironwork table on the terrace. Setting out the plates and dishes, Arielle poured out a glass of wine for Lycos, but none for herself, instead sticking to water.

Lycos, taking his place as she took hers, glanced at her.

Arielle looked at him limpidly. 'I must be picky about cheese, too,' she said. 'Nothing unpasteurised.'

Lycos frowned. She met his gaze, her expression still limpid. Then, as the penny dropped, Lycos surged to his feet, coming around the table.

'Oh, my God,' he breathed. 'Are you…? When did you…? I mean…' he rambled incoherently.

Arielle took his hand. 'Yes,' she said. 'And I found out this morning. Tested positive.'

Greek words broke from him, as they still did in times of great emotion. And what time of greater emotion, Arielle thought fondly as Lycos hunkered down beside her, throwing his arms around her and wrapping her in a bear hug, could be more deserving than to discover the greatest blessing of all was to be bestowed upon them?

'Next Easter, I reckon,' Arielle said, dropping a kiss on his head.

He got to his feet, his hand crushing hers. His night-dark eyes bored into hers.

'How is it possible to be even happier than we already are?' he said, his heart in his voice.

She smiled, lovingly, affectionately, understandingly, for the very same question was in her own head.

'I don't know. But this I do know.' She grazed his knuckle with her lips and lifted her gaze to his. 'That we give thanks, Lycos. We give thanks.'

She heard her voice catch and Lycos heard it too. And

with the same catch in his own voice, he bent to kiss her soft lips.

'We give thanks,' he echoed.

Arielle's heart swelled. Yes, they would give thanks, both of them, next Easter *all* of them, for all that they had been blessed with.

So very, very much...

* * * * *

Were you blown away by the drama in Dimistrios's Bought Mistress? *Then why not explore these other sensational stories by Julia James!*

The Heir She Kept from the Billionaire
Greek's Temporary Cinderella
Vows of Revenge
Accidental One-Night Baby
Marriage Made in Hate

Available now!

Get up to 4 Free Books!

We'll send you 2 free books from each series you try PLUS a free Mystery Gift.

FREE Value Over **$25**

Both the **Harlequin Presents** and **Harlequin Medical Romance** series feature exciting stories of passion and drama.

YES! Please send me 2 FREE novels from Harlequin Presents or Harlequin Medical Romance and my FREE gift (gift is worth about $10 retail). After receiving them, if I don't wish to receive any more books, I can return the shipping statement marked "cancel." If I don't cancel, I will receive 6 brand-new larger-print novels every month and be billed just $7.19 each in the U.S., or $7.99 each in Canada, or 4 brand-new Harlequin Medical Romance Larger-Print books every month and be billed just $7.19 each in the U.S. or $7.99 each in Canada, a savings of 20% off the cover price. It's quite a bargain! Shipping and handling is just 50¢ per book in the U.S. and $1.25 per book in Canada.* I understand that accepting the 2 free books and gift places me under no obligation to buy anything. I can always return a shipment and cancel at any time. The free books and gift are mine to keep no matter what I decide.

Choose one:
- ☐ **Harlequin Presents Larger-Print** (176/376 BPA G36Y)
- ☐ **Harlequin Medical Romance** (171/371 BPA G36Y)
- ☐ **Or Try Both!** (176/376 & 171/371 BPA G36Z)

Name (please print)

Address   Apt. #

City   State/Province   Zip/Postal Code

Email: Please check this box ☐ if you would like to receive newsletters and promotional emails from Harlequin Enterprises ULC and its affiliates. You can unsubscribe anytime.

Mail to the Harlequin Reader Service:
IN U.S.A.: P.O. Box 1341, Buffalo, NY 14240-8531
IN CANADA: P.O. Box 603, Fort Erie, Ontario L2A 5X3

Want to explore our other series or interested in ebooks? Visit www.ReaderService.com or call 1-800-873-8635.

---

*Terms and prices subject to change without notice. Prices do not include sales taxes, which will be charged (if applicable) based on your state or country of residence. Canadian residents will be charged applicable taxes. Offer not valid in Quebec. This offer is limited to one order per household. Books received may not be as shown. Not valid for current subscribers to the Harlequin Presents or Harlequin Medical Romance series. All orders subject to approval. Credit or debit balances in a customer's account(s) may be offset by any other outstanding balance owed by or to the customer. Please allow 4 to 6 weeks for delivery. Offer available while quantities last.

Your Privacy—Your information is being collected by Harlequin Enterprises ULC, operating as Harlequin Reader Service. For a complete summary of the information we collect, how we use this information and to whom it is disclosed, please visit our privacy notice located at https://corporate.harlequin.com/privacy-notice. Notice to California Residents – Under California law, you have specific rights to control and access your data. For more information on these rights and how to exercise them, visit https://corporate.harlequin.com/california-privacy. For additional information for residents of other U.S. states that provide their residents with certain rights with respect to personal data, visit https://corporate.harlequin.com/other-state-residents-privacy-rights/.

HPHM25